Robert McGuiness was born in Bayshore New York. He attended school in Smithtown and graduated from Smithtown High School in 1972. He made his way to the West Coast in 1976 and has made Northern California his home ever since . He enjoyed being a "Back to the Lander" and lived remotely, off grid. He has two children, Jewel and Bob, and a dog named Marbles. Currently he is involved with an Oak Restoration project, and associate of the Josephine Porter Institute for Applied Biodynamics. and a member of the North American Lily Society. When not busy he writes and studies and enjoys music.

Jewel and Bob my children and Sandra Chomicki their mother (1954-1987).

Robert McGuiness

DROPPED CALLS

AUSTIN MACAULEY PUBLISHERS™

LONDON • CAMBRIDGE • NEW YORK • SHARJAH

Ordering Information
Quantity sales: Special discounts are available on quantity purchases by corporations, associations, and others. For details, contact the publisher at the address below.

Publisher's Cataloging-in-Publication data
McGuiness, Robert
Dropped Calls

ISBN 9798886934717 (Paperback)
ISBN 9798886934724 (Hardback)
ISBN 9798886934748 (ePub e-book)
ISBN 9798886934731 (Audiobook)

Library of Congress Control Number: 2023917361

www.austinmacauley.com/us

First Published 2024
Austin Macauley Publishers LLC
40 Wall Street, 33rd Floor, Suite 3302
New York, NY 10005
USA

mail-usa@austinmacauley.com
+1 (646) 5125767

5G Over Walden Pond

"Put your cellphone down," I said out loud to myself…but could I? Like telling a child, 'Stay out of the cookie jar', all they hear is 'cookie jar', 'Don't do drugs' is how the D.A.R.E. program helped create the opioid epidemic. If one were to Google bad habits or compulsive behaviors there, you would find me scrolling down into the sunset…plaster it on your Facebook to get a million likes and a twitter long-sleeved tee.

The night before last, I had a dream, which I thought was a message from God. One cellphone was telling another cellphone, "Put that person down. They will make you stupid. Do you know you're not even supposed to be holding a person while you're on that app." AI, Artificial Ignorance, steeped in my psyche, manifesting in cold sweats and night terrors.

When that little voice in my head comes from clear across the universe, I not only take notice…I take action. I decided I needed to get away. Away, away from all the noise and lights. Far from the 'conveniences' of the modern world. With hopes of being able to restore my ability to think, to plan, and execute within the guidelines of the moral compass in which I had been raised. It wasn't too late for me, and I hoped not too late for the species.

Fantasizing about a simpler life, I became cultured and sophisticated about the process of shedding all the unnecessary from my life. Looking around the house, every direction brought grief and decision.

This had to be a clean break, a parting with emotion and memory. Discard the replications collected through years of building comfort and home. Perhaps the future would once again allow me to be coddled with possessions; for now, I had to be honest with myself and truthful in my quest for simplicity. I could think. I could wait. I could fast. As I stripped myself from attachment, it dawned on me how much I had to carry. Not very funny, but a running joke of all the noise inside one's head. The incredible banks of information accumulated over a life. *The Odyssey, The Bible, Trailer Park Boys, The Jerk,* my capacity for remembering the input was as stellar as the ability to discern the art from the crap.

As I had recently immersed myself in Greek Classics, I could not help but think of Henry David Thoreau and what he thought about writing as the pinnacle of the arts. How as the sculptures and paintings eroded and faded over time, the classics remained and continued to shine with brilliance and seasoned patina over the millennium. Walden Pond or somewhere nearby would be my domicile, my retreat into the past, my kingdom in a bubble. Escape the lethal social environs that presented the corona virus and coaxed us to a doom with cellphones and Pornhub. It was still unknown…was God mean? Would he be mean to me? If I rejected and distanced myself from what man had judged to be sin, would that satisfy a God? If a man, in whatever slice of society, was in the position to be judge would he speak to and for God? There was only retreat and listen. Wait, and think and fast for God would eventually speak directly to me even if the conversations were difficult to live with and assimilate into my own humble being.

The friends and almost constant companionship would be the hardest to part from. Most of them did not take me seriously and assumed I would be back in a week. Taking weekend backpacking trips was fairly routine, but they didn't see me as one who would pull up stakes and leave all the comforts behind. Sarah was expecting us to be married by end of spring and though I had her blessings, she was not happy. We had a plan and she was to meet me later when I had made a comfortable space. I didn't have the liberty of just building a cabin like my predecessor. My camp was going to have to be humbler and more temporary and was still needing to provide some comforts for an urbanite like Sarah.

Those thoughts like cloud cover were not an obex to sunshine.

The break was clean and abrupt. The planning primitive and childlike. David willingly was coerced into making the six-hour drive north with me and my few bundles of stuff. There was no science or philosophy rolling around my head but an altruistic zest, a liberating sensation of floating in an ever-expanding universe. Not just any universe but my self-made universe as vast and dark and frightening and yet as warm and full of light as any of the others. We listened to the Grateful Dead as we drove into new territory. The music distanced me from where I had been and gave me strength and a sense of solidarity. After some great Jerry riffs, we were singing along with 'I will survive' and it dawned on me how much noise it would take to get away from noise. I was just a couple hours away from quiet, and I was going to be loud, now, while I could. "I will get by."

We traveled down the Concord Road to where the Baker Bridge Road met. This was the stepping-off point to a trip back in time, to a life more simply lived. The pocket watch Sarah had given me I thought would be safer back at home, besides I didn't want to know the time unless I could get back my natural sense of it and I handed it over to David. "Keep good care of it. Have Sarah hold it for me."

I wrestled my pack out of the SUV and laughing, said to David, "I will see you when the world calms down."

David said over the blasting music, "That ain't happening!" He handed me a couple of bandanas, a little bag of weed and a couple of painkillers… "just in case you fall into a vortex." After a moment, he was gone, and I was standing alone on the side of the road. I had read a map and knew the trail to Adams Woods was right here, and in the pre-moon, darkness made my way into the woods. I didn't make a camp just got far enough out of site and rolled my bag out listening closely to my new environment. 'I will survive' echoed till the deep hours when I finally dozed off.

Morning was filled with life and it was such a welcome change to the routine I had back home. There are some withdrawal symptoms to shedding the dependency of my cell phone addiction. Oh, it wasn't because I needed to talk to someone…but to look stuff up or for emergencies. I was jonesing, but I was clean and signal less and I was getting through it. Today was the day to retreat into a bield among the brambles and distance myself from the twenty-first century. There was difficulties in maintaining that balance between being comfortable enough to think and write and being on edge hearing something or think you are hearing something. I navigated the tightrope. The plan was to stay as long as possible and only move if I had been discovered or if someone had discovered the camp. There was no need to keep an eye on the road or the trails, so getting far off of them and down in a gulch instead of seeking the open vantage point higher up the hill. Wanting to be near Walden pond had me heading in an easterly direction off the trail. The trail had its fair share of visitors so I needed to be quiet and stealth at all times.

After making a lean-to, I viewed it from all angles. Nothing man-made was visible, the camouflage helped remove all the unnatural lines of my new domicile. Setting up a few warning systems allowed me to know if someone was approaching or had been there while I was gone. If I was out on the trails, I wanted to look like a casual day hiker and not a homeless squatter. It was important to be neat…I was always keeping up appearances. I had lugged my collapsible water container up with me so I knew I was good for several days. Scouting around, I found a spring nearby; there was also water from spigots and faucets inside the park. The water in my jug actually came from the park. I had filled it there before David had dropped me off.

The woods were quiet and beautiful. My eagerness to be a part of that natural state separated me from it. It would take some time to ebb and flow with the natural rhythm. For that first twenty-four hours, I did not see a soul, not one for the first time in almost a decade. I had heard a couple of people down on the trail and, in the distance, I could hear vehicles, but I saw no one. That night I looked at the stars through the broken canopy. Never more than a minute or two and a plane or satellite would pass through my field of vision. I thought Thoreau never had that kind of noise or interruptions. I thought how absurd my quest for a life lived more simply while hiding in a park with jets and satellites invading my solitude and complicating my simple. Since my childhood, I was always planting seeds of ideas before I sleep, trying to direct dreams or solve problems in my subconscious state. If I wrote a problem or thought down and fell off to sleep, I could never connect that thought to my dreams, but when I first wake up and read the note and fall back to sleep, there would be clarity and many times resolve.

Tonight the simple entry read… "you are free, keep it simple." I thought a few good nights of acclimating to the quiet and solitude would be good. I could see where my dreams would take me without trying to direct or misinterpret them. I wrote briefly in my journal of the spot, the lean-to, the spring and fell off into a deep undisturbed slumber.

The next couple of days were spent exploring my surroundings. The lake itself I circled in both directions and of course visited the cabin site and the visitors center. The geological and hydrological maps were packed with details about the nature of the place, and I thought how far man had come in a century and a half. Information down to atoms of the rocks, the soils, the waters, the life, all at the touch of a button. Weather and patterns of weather recorded and all accessible. The complete solitude was scarce or actually not at all and my distracted soul yearned for what no longer existed. Even as I preoccupied myself with the forest's stratification and noted and listed species, the not-too-distant heartbeat of civilization sounded its uninhibited drum and horn. I was proud of the fact I had left my phone behind…but of course there were times I really believed I needed it, my own drum and horn.

Efforts were made to no avail to deny myself of some fundamental building blocks which are the foundation of the person that developed from those precision-cut stones. Though I am Christian, there had been many days spent reading and studying other philosophies, other religions. The thoughts and behaviors of years of indoctrination, of fellowship, guided my every thought and move. To know if God was gentle or mean, to even reintroduce myself to God as an adult, I needed to banish my former self and distance myself from him. For now, I would reject all I learned of philosophies, all I learned of religion, all I knew from and of man and simply live observing nature searching for the clues that allowed me to belong. My mind would race from thought to thought and even my thoughts to myself were in a language too sophisticated for Australopithecus. I thought of Jane Goodall trying to convey green to a great ape. Having zero vocabulary at least in a human sense and yet still having enough knowledge to not only survive but to have order in a society and in family, to raise their young, teach them how to find food and avoid danger. I worked on making observations without language. These would become my strongest asset as these were true gifts of personal knowledge.

There was a well that was closer to the pond and not far from camp that I called Beer after a well in the old testament…I also thought it funny to be going out for a beer every day and washing my dishes in Beer. Even things as simple as the water separated me from my primitive ancestors. The Beer was a blessing. It never occurred to me to wonder what was in it or to have it tested for minerals or contaminants; it was always cool and tasteless and refreshing, water. Not once did I think I needed to boil it. The Beer water was truly a blessing, and I acknowledged it as such and gave thanks.

The weather was still cool, the nights crisp and clear. In the big moon, there were as many satellites as stars. There were encouraging signs of spring as every branch and blade were summoned from above. There was a calm and comfort emerging, and I felt content in being able to be. My internal noise fell into the hum of external sounds and was the beginning of my belonging.

The night was cut short, morning came early. There was extra activity in my neck of the woods. Grabbing some trail mix and fruit, I decided to hunker down by the main trail and see what was going on while trying not to give my camp location away. I could hear footsteps getting closer and now the voices were quite clear. I should have put my camp up, I thought to myself. From off the trail coming down the hill behind me just northerly from my camp, I hear, "Good morning."

Turning to see who was there, I replied, "Good morning."

"I need you to stay right where you are," he said with a tone of total authority. He was uniformed and looked like a state trooper to me.

I am thinking…busted, I am going to have to pay some fines and find a new camping spot.

"Keep your hands where I can see them!" he said with even more troubling a tone, more aggressive, more hostile. I was used to getting treated like a useless feeder back home so I was expecting the same.

"What can I do for you?" I calmly asked.

"Were you here last night?" he asked, a little less agitated.

"Yes, I was," I responded, knowing not to lie especially to an obviously agro cop on a mission.

"You know you are not allowed to camp here?"

"Yes, sir," I responded. "I am working on finding a more permanent place. I am studying sociology and examining the intricacies of social distancing in terms of time rather than physical space."

"You are going to have to come with me down to the station," he said civilly. Then from the ravine, there was a shout, "Over here, over here! We got something."

Immediately I knew it was my camp they had found. I wasn't sweating it. I had already resigned to the fact I would have to rebuild. The officer that had me detained was Officer McCullough, and I told him, "I think that's my stuff up there."

"Should we go take a look?" he asked.

"Okay," I said. "I'd like to keep my sleeping bag and my pack," I told him.

By now the harshness had eased, and I don't think he felt threatened by me. His fellow officers seemed all pumped up, and I was having trouble believing this was how the fascist dealt with illegal campers.

I expected all my things to be destroyed when we walked up there, or heaped in a pile to be removed, instead they taped off the area and not one thing had been touched. There was more to this than trespassing, and I started to get that sinking feeling, started to worry.

"What is going on?" nervously asking.

"We'll let you know. Did you see or hear anything that we should know about?" he asked without giving me any clues.

"No," I answered after a short pause.

"Let's go," he said. "Your stuff is going to have to stay here for the time being."

I felt really lucky they didn't even cuff me. We walked south on the Adams Woods Trail to where he had a car waiting. Next I knew, we were in the station house, and it was abuzz. I was left alone in a room and sat there for a couple of hours. They checked me out and found I was who I said I was and had only a minor marijuana charge in my past. Still I could tell something was not adding up for them…of course, I thought it was always like that. When they brought me into another room where lots of people busy at their desks were working, I heard the words "body mutilated, horrific." Again, that sinking feeling. I saw Officer McCullough talking to the captain. I caught his eye and when I got a chance, I asked, "Did someone get murdered." He told me someone had but that was all.

I was escorted into a holding cell, and there were a couple of other folks in there. I looked at them all as possible murderers and tried not to be an irritant. Same old same old, at least one was not to be trusted. The intimidator is always suspect. They held me as long as was allowed even with their extensions, and I was glad to be released. They didn't have any evidence to charge me with a crime, let alone convicting me of anything. I knew I was at their mercy and was thankful for my release. My camp had been thoroughly combed over and examined, but to my surprise, all my stuff was still there. I had told the investigating detective that I would be around and I would check in, but it was time to break camp and move to greener pastures. As I was breaking down my lean-to and gathering my belongings, I tried to envision the path forward. To live a life more simply was becoming humorous, really started believing it was not possible and was perhaps my personal greatest folly. The more I tried to distance myself from the external noise...the louder the internal noise...and vice versa.

Walking the trail to the northwest, I chose another bield in heavy brush. City living has a way of hardening one off, and I never felt threatened or in danger. Maybe it was a sense of faith, maybe apathy. I wasn't going to lose any sleep over it. I heard about the murder that recently happened right near here. The body was hacked into little pieces that were neatly arranged in an organized grouping. The severed head was left on the top of the remains facing up. The site was somewhere between a half mile and a mile away, closer to the highway and closer to Walden Pond itself. What was bothering me was getting locked up and having to move my camp.

After I settled in, I ate some food and turned in. My sleep was deep and peaceful, my dreams nonsense and seemingly random fragments of nonlinear thought. How one can feel so rested after a night of that is beyond me, but I woke up happy and energized and ready for another stellar day. The day flew by, making my camp more comfortable and hidden. A small drainage ditch would help keep running water away, and a couple of logs were sufficient table enough to keep my belongings off the ground. Granola and gorp kept my energy level up and my belly from growling. It was towards dusk that a loud commotion was heard about a hundred or so yards to the west. I swiftly and quietly made my way in that direction. As I passed through a small break in the canopy, I could see the tree line in the next stand. In the treetops, a group of frantic squirrels were jumping from one tree to another squealing. As I watched, it became evident there were not two sides to the fight but every squirrel was fighting every other squirrel. There were seven that I could count and the treetops were swinging and bending to the point of breaking. On one upper branch a squirrel getting bitten by several others made his last cry and fell like a rock and lay lifeless on the forest floor twenty-five or thirty feet in front me. The remaining squirrels seemed to emerge from their trance and scattered in all directions. I wondered how rare it was to see such behavior. Was this the privilege of those who commune with nature? The natural world is brutal, but something seemed wrong and completely unnatural. It bothered me as I walked back to camp in the growing silence and the growing darkness. From the jug of spring water I filled from the spring by the camp, I made a cold tea and I cherry picked my gorp eating only the hazelnuts and pieces of dates. I thought it funny how each time I cherry picked my gorp, I had a different ingredient as my favorite. As I went to sleep, I realized how much the squirrels creeped me out. I kept my flashlight in my hand and pulled my sleeping bag full over my head. I must have lay there two hours before I fell asleep.

The next morning I was glad there were no witnesses. I found myself about a quarter mile from camp. I was completely naked and covered in blood. My legs had a thousand cuts and my feet were sore and punctured. My hands were bloody. I didn't know where I had been or what I had been doing. I wondered if it wasn't I who was the murderer. I knew someone had been murdered right near here. So I knew the murderer was right here…I just didn't know if I was that murderer. Yesterday and the day before I knew I wasn't, but today the possibility was great, perhaps even a probability. I was relieved I was alone and yet I was greatly disturbed, losing control, losing command of my vessel.

I returned to the spring on my way back to camp and scrubbed as much as I could. I had no idea what kind of blood I was covered in or where it came from. Trying to remove all traces, I threw new leaves in and around the spring. As I gathered from around the area, I found a half dozen dead birds and a dead rabbit. I'd say nothing was more than five days dead. Hearing distant voices reminded me of my nakedness, and I headed back to camp.

Camp was totally undisturbed and a comfort to me. Whatever happened, happened away from camp? Hopefully, it was still a safe place. I took out my pen and notebook and made a pact with myself to write everything down. No matter how insignificant or trivial, I needed to log as many moments as I could and see where the gaps were and if there would be a pattern. From that moment on, everything I ate or drank was noted.

I was trying to remember and journal all my dreams. Trying to keep track of my emotions and how often they would change, and if identifying triggers could be associated with those changes. There would be no mutiny on this bounty. I thought today I should fast, as a clean slate is an appropriate place to start self-investigation. I would fast maybe three or four days and check the emotional rhythms and the clarity and focus of attention on cerebral pursuits. I knew this starting point was pure chaos, and there was a lot to reel in. It would be difficult to think about anything other than what the hell happened to me and was it going to happen again. I was familiar with brain dysfunction and dementia...too soon? Could I ever really trust myself again? As I festered on my own shortcomings, feelings of aggression and violence swept over me. My thoughts, like light through a prism, separated and took off in different directions. There suddenly was no calm. Agitated, I headed off southwest towards one of the lakes. Walking rapidly with great strides and power. Grabbing rocks and small stones along the way, I was throwing them at birds or squirrels, not even like a hunter, just like an asshole killing or breaking things. Random completely out-of-character acts without reason. Though I wanted to keep track of these very behaviors I didn't write a single word. There was no way I could even begin to express how I felt, nor did I want any evidence of, or to claim any responsibility for these damning acts.

As I came upon the lake, I finally started to breathe easier. It was still, quiet and serene. The sky was a rich dark blue, an occasional soft white cloud would float by and I could see its reflected image in the water. I wondered why suddenly I didn't want to throw a rock at that fluffy cloud on the still waters. I struggled with ideas of how to keep control of myself. It seemed such a major accomplishment being content for the moment. I wasn't throwing rocks. Was my life going to inch by in guarded position? I stepped out of the trees near the east side of the lake where a beaten path hugged the shore and circled the water. My eyes scanned the pastoral scene and looking to the south shore a bright glare taxed my eyes and I couldn't see but blue and green dots for a moment. I moved down the trail to the south to see what was there. Before I even got to the south bank, a stench of rotting flesh wafted in my direction. I could see now there were thousands of dead fish on the shore and in the path. The sun played off their silver bodies and burned the image in my memory. They didn't appear to be dead from an oil spill or the like where they may float up and turn belly up pushed against the pond edge opposite the water inlet, or blown into a mass by a wind. They actually surrounded the entire lake fairly well. At first, I thought they were expelled at the high-water mark, but I dismissed that idea as there was no other debris and no recent set high water mark. Moving a little further from the water I continued my way around the lake. At the stream that was the inlet to the lake there were many dead fish. As I looked back to the east the white and silver pathway made a beautiful eerie collage. The birds were chattering away making extra noise adding a dramatic edge to an otherwise serene landscape. A bullfrog was devouring another bullfrog and for a split second I wished I had my phone so I could take a picture.

Circling on back to the trail to camp I ran into another hiker on the trail. He was to guess, about thirty years old. He was clean and neat. He had light red brown hair and a trimmed beard. I could tell he was professional, just wasn't sure of the profession. After saying hello he told me his name was Robert. He was a biologist.

"There are thousands of dead fish up ahead. It is an amazing sight!" I told him excited like a little kid, it had been a couple of days since I had human contact.

"I know, that is why I am here. I was told it was a mass suicide…but I am not convinced of that, so I am doing my own investigation," he said calmly. "Does that happen?" I asked.

"It has happened before, but it is usually because of some environmental anomaly, low oxygen levels, pesticides. We've documented beaching of whales from sonar. We don't believe they were suicidal just misguided…same result," he said matter of fact.

"Wow," I said with a loss for all other words.

Just then his phone started with one of those factory jingles and I bid him good day and good luck.

On my way back to my camp I thought of how much the word suicide really bothered me. So violent and final and yet so much in control. I thought what if you did it when you didn't have control…what a tragic loss. That word in the morning sucks even more. Just imagine being on psyche meds where your demons are prescribed to you and authorities stand over to make sure they are administered. Happy little fish kills.

I wrote quite a bit that day. I tried to keep tabs on myself, so I wrote about the fish kill and the biologist. Had a few dream remnants written out. I wrote about the birds I saw and any plants that were exciting or unusual…but all in all it was a rather dry read. The woods had an eerie quiet that evening, and I was hoping for a restful night. I ate ginger snaps, peanut butter and apples until I was content. For some reason my gut told me not to drink the water and I sipped on some juice I had. As I looked up at the sky I looked towards the darkest emptiest place, staring until I would see a star there. It is something I always did when I was younger. Funny how no matter where you look sooner or later a star appears. Tonight in the void between stars I would see a satellite making its orbit and in my quiet outrage I would extend a middle finger. By midnight I was clenching my teeth with both middle fingers extended, dreaming of a life lived simply.

What a relief it was the next morning when I woke up where I went to bed and I was still in the same clothes. I could remember my dreams of being in a car on a draw bridge, and one about being in some unknown room with a friend I hadn't seen in more than a decade. It was nice to have normalcy returned and it set the tone for a good day with positive vibes. Today I was going to go into town and pick up a few supplies. But I also wanted to speak to officer McCullough and see if I could get anything from him on the murder. I didn't expect much from him but I was going to see what I could get. I ate a couple handfuls of granola, camouflaged my spot and got right on the road. My first stop was beer and I needed to fill my water jugs, which I did and stashed them near the road. I hitched a ride with an elderly man who was nice enough to stop. He was going all the way into town and if I was around the diner at two, he could take me back. I wasn't sure I'd be there then and told him so…don't wait if I 'm not there. His name was Ben and lived there his entire life of seventy-three years. He knew everything about Walden and in fact Massachusetts. I asked him if he heard about the murder up there and he said he had. He also said, "the woods have been very strange recently." He observed some of the same anomalies I had with animals attacking each other, plants growing deformed or dying off.

"In all my life I've never seen more bizarre and brutal behavior. I don't know what is causing it, but it is getting progressively worse. I am afraid to walk Walden Pond at this point and I have walked it for seventy years" he added.

"I'll be poking around to see if I can't find out what's going on", I reassured him. In no time we rolled into town and I hopped out thanking him for the ride. I told him if I missed the ride back, I would look for him in the future and he seemed glad at least someone was looking into the natural disturbances I wanted to shop last thing before heading back so I went to the precinct to find officer McCullough. It wasn't but a minute after walking into the precinct that I spotted Officer McCullough. He appeared to be in a hurry and agitated. He was behind the large desk in the entrance way to another busy room, and talking to a small lean older man. The older man looked distinguished and spoke with some sort of eastern European accent. I overheard the name Dr. Armich coming from Officer McCullough and assumed that was whom he was speaking with. I am not sure if it is because he was a Dr. or because he was several decades my senior but he seemed brilliant. He seemed to know more English language or at least more vocabulary than anyone I knew. My guess was he was seventy-five years old. He was probably five foot six or seven in height, thin like one hundred twenty-five or thirty pounds. He seemed healthy and moved with grace and ease. His thin gray hair was receding, and he had his thin yarns combed over.

From talking to the desk sergeant I learned he was doing forensic work on the victim by the lake. He was exceptionally good at what he did and the demand for him seemed to be proliferating. Waving my hand I caught Officer McCullough's attention. I was surprised when he came right over.

"How are you?" I asked.

"Well, thank you and yourself? I am really busy; is there something you need?" he said patiently.

"I just wanted to know if there were any suspects yet on the lake case?" I asked nervously.

"No, no suspects yet. We identified the victim as thirty-two-year-old Anthony Petercelli," he said as a matter of fact.

"Any clues?" I added.

"Yes, but I am not at liberty to discuss those." He added with a professional demeanor.

"Am I on the list?" I blurted out nervously. I could not believe I asked that, but I had to know.

I don't know if he was joking, but he looked at my feet and asked, "What size shoe do you wear?"

"Nine," I answered.

"No, you're not on the list," he said, but I still couldn't tell if he was serious and it didn't bring me any sense of comfort.

He walked back over to where Dr. Armich was standing and they talked for several minutes. I could hear part of what they were saying…the victim was a regular with a long rap sheet. He had a couple robberies but mostly drug- and alcohol-related charges, DUI, public intoxication, disturbing the peace, possessions. It seemed anyone that knew him expected a premature, violent death, or some type of 'accidental' suicide. I heard Dr. Armich say he recognized that smell and for some reason I just assumed it was meth.

Officer McCullough looked over at me, and I waved again and left.

Though I wasn't that long, I missed my ride back. Hitching took longer than I had hoped. Standing on the side of the road, waiting for of all things, a car to drive me off to a simpler life. The entire scene agitated me, but there I was walking, sticking out my thumb at every chance for a ride when a car drove by. I thought about the police station, for some reason, the big clock on the wall barked at me. I already felt taxed with the numerous phones and monitors and the full array of florescent lights, but that clock not only kept me from enlightenment but seemed to be keeping score as well. It would say things like "look at the time, are you there yet" or "look another unenlightened hour went by" and "you're wasting your life."

The time for meditating was long overdue, and it was hard to believe I had drifted this far from my spiritual self. In my quest, I lost my Zen; in my quiet I made noise; in my ignorance, my transcendental state was illusions of a lost soul. I found myself outside of myself and intellectually planning how to get 'me' back. I remembered when I just used to be, it was simple, it was spontaneous, it was real. There was going to be a long silence, and if a thought arose, it could not be about me. Being in service always shifted the focal point away from oneself. I concentrated on Anthony Petercelli, hoping to see a glimpse or catch a clue, and I found myself praying for him and his family.

I think I walked a couple of miles before I got a ride to the pond. Deal and Me and My Uncle were dominating the space between my ears. Back in camp I was glad to have left town behind and let the solitude empower me and the quiet direct me. It darkened quickly that night and the woods again became noisy and unsettled. Sitting with my back straight I breathed deep and purposefully, counting at first and then devolving to thoughts of nothing. From time to time, a screech or wail would infiltrate my Zen, and I would scramble back to the void. It was difficult to sleep that night as the stimuli from town and the breathing were both energizing. Eventually I fell off to sleep, listening, just listening to the universe through my dreams.

Before breakfast, I walked east and south to another small pond. Determined to realize the simple life, I walked off unprepared, ready to test my resourcefulness and my strengths. There was an unusual peace and calm. There was a silence in the woods, which was kind of eerie. The smells of earth and water and greenery enriched my vitality and cleansed my mind. Expecting to see a mass of fish on the shores I was surprised and curios to find not a one. Sitting in a partially shaded nook facing the pond I started breathing slowly, deeply, in and out, clearing my mind. There had been an anxiousness building to find the time to meditate and finally I had arrived and with great comfort and satisfaction I was in that position where I could listen to the universe, where I could become the universe. As I dissipated and mingled visions of salts appeared and would demand action and not acceptance. Zen would not allow me to know these things and not see them as problems. Right or wrong, yes and no, life and death our simplistic binary reality could not separate itself from the duality(s) of our existence. There was a cry I heard from the universe that day. There was an urgent call to duty. All of life on the planet was at risk, the cause of which was the fact all of our water was at risk. I was given no further clues or directions. As I sat, I thought perhaps some chemical imbalance led me to this altruistic mindset. The message was so loud I could not return to thoughts of nothingness and my self-disturbing mind put much effort into just that. I did feel a sense of accomplishment in that I cleared my mind and talked to the universe and very loudly it spoke back to me. There was a newfound purpose. The complexity of simple was far more than any human could understand, or should comprehend.

As I walked back to camp, I thought about the pond and my fleeting enlightenment. Some of those thoughts and feelings I put into words and was anxious to record them in my notes...

The Ripple (Fleeting Enlightenment)

By the reflecting pond my master sits.
Still, on the mirrored glass he sees his face.
Perhaps a thousand seasons came and went.
Another autumn of blushing maples.

Pulsing ebb and flow of rushing silence,
the master generates an ancient calm.
His reflection becomes more real than I.
In the pond, all that moves, clouds floating by.

A turtle or fish, or dragonfly dips,
the pane with the image is distorted.
How small a mind to catch such large a thought…
as I and the ripple in the water.

As the sky before me would undulate,
the ripple painted lines across the plate,
the sky above the water below
following divides, where I dissipate.

How large a mind to catch such small a thought.
My original face not seen again.
The ripple, the pond, the sky are all one.
By the reflecting pond my master sits.

The day wasted no time transitioning into night. I thought I would eat and turn in fairly early. As I reached for my water container, I remembered I hadn't filled it. I raced the darkness to the closest spring and filled it up. Thoughts of my conversation with the universe echoed in my mind. All the water, all the life…what did this cryptic, ominous communique mean. Tonight I would put that on the tip of my mind and sleep on it.

What vestige of innocence remains in the grown child surfaces as he surrenders to sleep and lays vulnerable to the haunting terrors that stalk such prey. This night offered no insights or resolutions. Before dawn, I was awakened by my own violent thrashings, screaming and inconsolable rage. Every muscle in my body was contracted, and I was drenched in sweat. I paced deliberately back and forth, fists clenched, teeth grinding, short, constricted breaths. My legs felt foreign and my feet were like two pier blocks hammering at the earth. I cursed at every thought I had, and damned the rising sun. After some long hours passed, I was slowly taking deeper breaths and started to relax my muscles. The rage was waning and my thoughts were coming back into focus. Pieces of dreams from the night before crystallized. Everything was wrong! I was a raindrop; an agoraphobic raindrop. The term may be aquaphobic rain drop. The terror was consuming and as I fell to earth, I had to avoid all other rain drops. I would die if I splashed into a puddle or ran down in a torrent out into the ocean. It seemed I spent half the night trying not to land. Dissipating so I could float, dodging drops, the angry drops that took on human traits, constantly seeking vengeance. Mean, hungry, aggressive cannibal drops whose only mission was to consume and to erase any identity.

Even as I recalled the pieces, I was shaking and damaged. I thought again…all the life…all the water. Once again, I had taken water from the spring and my sleep was so disturbing, I would spend days questioning my mental health and trying to reverse the self-propelling spiral into insanity. I had to stand by insisting I was not crazy and dig for proof to explain and justify such erratic behaviors and untethered thoughts.

Hearing voices over on the trail brought me back around. Too much time alone makes it difficult to gauge normal. I walked over to the trail and said, "Good morning." It was a young family, thirty-ish, with three children. The oldest was probably six or seven and the littlest was in a pack. We talked for a moment, and it was reassuring to see normal and to feel normal.

After returning to camp, I ate a small cup of dried cereal. I was determined to get peace back in my life. I knew I wasn't reacting to the news or social media or influenced by a mob. I wasn't on drugs or raging from alcohol. This seemed to have natural and organic etiology, which just did not feel right.

The plan for today was to get back into town. I was going to go to a lab and get some specimen bottles and test some of the waters. There had been growing suspicions of the spring water I had used on several occasions. I found it easy to come up with all sorts of theories, and conspiracies, but proving them or eliminating them was a whole different reality show.

As soon as I made my way to the pavement, I got a ride. I was lucky he was going all the way to where I wanted to go. He told me his name was John but went by JJ or Junior.

"You come from the lake?" he asked.

"Yeah. I've been going there a lot lately," I said not wanting to reveal I was staying there.

"It's been kind of freaky lately. I wonder what's been going on there?" he said.

"Why do you say that?" I asked to hear what he would say, see if l could get any more insight.

"For one, there has been a lot of dead birds and a lot of dead fish. No signs of spilt oil or any news of DDT showing up in tests," he said knowledgably.

I was glad to hear this, but it didn't solve any problems. I did feel like I was in good company. As we continued our conversation, I learned he was a descendant of John Audobon. He wasn't named for him but his name 'Junior' was a tribute to the footprints he walked in. He was a naturalist and an ornithologist.

"I had to get a degree…every time I had a bird or feather, I was breaking the law. The charges were piling up when I was a kid. Once I got busted for having a pileated woodpecker feather tethered to my roach clip. I kept trying to gather specimens of all the rare birds to paint and study…well, we can't be having that!" he said adamantly pissed but still in humorous spirits.

"What brings you here?" I asked.

"I had read about birds dying off in one of my journals. I had to come see for myself and see what could be done," he said professionally and solemnly.

"That's pretty cool," I said like an idiot. "I've had a few thoughts of my own. I was by one of the other ponds the other day and it looked like every single fish jumped out of the water there. The reason I am going to town today is to get sample containers to test some of the waters," I said with a swelling ego.

"What do you expect to find?" JJ asked.

"I really don't know, but I think the water has something to do with all the strange things going on.

"I was thinking maybe metals because they can interfere with the ability to control or inhibit behaviors. Whatever it is, things are just reacting, even to their own demise. Hopefully, we find at least a clue to what would attack the foundations of normal biologic systems."

"Metals…that's interesting…I'm not sure how much of that human behavior you can pass back to the simpler life forms. One has to do a lot of thinking and reasoning to inhibit behaviors, not that metals couldn't have an effect across the spectrum. Maybe it isn't water related…could be a virus or bacteria," he added, broadening the field.

The lab was in Medford Massachusetts, and JJ was kind enough to drive me to the door. He was highly motivated and waited for me. I returned with six sample bottles, which I thought would be a good start. I wanted to test two springs and two wells and two pond sites. We grabbed lunch and stopped for a few supplies and then headed back. JJ lit a joint he pulled out of his pocket and put Birdsong on. I drifted off into some manic paradise, comforted in those familiar things, and instantaneously JJ was family and we were kin to every living thing. It was a great honor to connect not just with JJ but to myself and to have direction and purpose that was appreciated and understood and encouraged. This is the type of stimulation that grooms genius.

We talked for a short while after returning to the pond. We made plans to meet up, and he was to give me a ride back to drop the sample bottles off at the lab. In the evening, I spent time pressing plant samples for my herbarium. I had collected several many cruciferous mustards and I was fascinated by the subtle changes in colors and the extent to which the palate was expressed. As I pressed the many-colored flowers into their pages, I couldn't help thinking about the water samples. Something I had learned in an ecology class as a youngster was how when the humidity rose and the barometer dropped certain tree leaves would flip, showing the underside. It would be an indicator of coming rain. Tonight I was thinking, what if when the barometer dropped and the humidity rose a person would flip. Be unpredictable, indicating a storm was approaching, perhaps not able to control his own behavior. The night passed quickly and quietly.

As the first light appeared, I was already tossing and turning. I lay there staring at the morning star and organizing my day. The birds were full of chatter and song, and I made an effort to orchestrate harmonies between the voicings. Knowing it was a full day for me I made a strong pot of coffee. I sipped it slow, looking into the cup at my reflected face and watching it distort as my heart beat. Then I would try to flatline and make the coffee in the cup as still as I possibly could. Slow and shallow breaths, this type of meditation always had a positive effect on my outlook and rejuvenated a sluggish spirit.

I prepared a small pack to take into town and got busy gathering water samples. As plain and as clear all the water samples looked, one of the samples from a spring just felt wrong. It looked the same and didn't have many noticeable particulates there was just a vibe about it that felt evil, to the point that I poured a little out over my fingers to see if it felt different. Nothing noticeable just a plastic bottle of water. It was not something one can easily discard and that 'evil' sample was the main focus of my attention for most of the day. Letting the early morning pass with my mind occupying and amusing itself, it was now time to gather my pack and head towards the main parking for Walden Pond.

JJ was already waiting for me when I made the parking area. "Morning! I hope I didn't keep you waiting long?" I said.

"Not at all…I just got here. Looks like another beautiful day. You got everything you need?" he said with a real concern for the research.

"Yeah, I think I got it all. When you start thinking too much, you sure want to take more samples with you. But we are fine for now," I told him.

As we were pulling out onto the road, I noticed a film on one edge of the parking area that extended into the grass and dirt areas to the east. It was a greyish in color and looked dusty, blanketing everything like a covering of pollen. I pointed it out to JJ; he didn't seem to know what it was either. There was a disturbing comfort in the distance from that life lived more simply…as the little glass and metal box sped along the turnpike with the mornings motivational bluegrass charging our souls and pumping fresh blood to our brains. The artificial stimulus certainly heightened the airs of altruism and crystallized the importance of these seemingly mundane tasks at hand. It also added appreciably to the common grounds and our friendship.

We stopped and got coffee and a Danish along the way. We were both firing on all cylinders, talking of almost anything…except…politics, religion, cars, sports…well we talked about a lot of (meaningful) stuff. For all the excitement I was in the Lab for about ten minutes. I dropped the samples off and that was that. We stopped at the store and picked a few things up but I was back at camp by noon. It would be several days to have the samples done so I was to call early the next week. JJ was going to come by next Tuesday morning, so we hoped to head back to Medford then.

As the weekend approached the visitors in the woods increased. In fact Saturday with its warmer weather and blue skies saw the most people since I had been here. Though I hung out by Walden Pond most of the day I was worried someone might stumble on my belongings. I had hidden them fairly well but still nervous they were unattended. I wondered if Thoreau was in a constant state of distrusting his fellow humans, or were things that much better back in time and out of the cities. Dicken's rascals don't usually come to mind thinking of Thoreau, but human nature has some timeless consistencies in its fundamental makeup.

Early the next morning I was awakened to sirens screaming up the turnpike. It was just barely light and the sirens were loud and persistent. It sounded as if the vehicles stopped before the noise was too distant to be heard. One morning banjoes one morning sirens and the simple life perhaps just a pipedream. The triggering sirens at dawn had me wishing for a scanner or my old cellphone to see what was going on. I didn't want to know, I needed to know. Taking a deep breath I said to myself and this too shall pass. I hate to think of Sarah in this light…triggers, cellphones, depression, Sarah. Of course in time of need, but she deserves banjoes and blue skies. As I groped for comfort, I wrote to her. Let her know what I had been up to and how there were more unanswered questions than answers. At this point a life more simply lived was actually associated with birth defects, and sociopathic anomalies.

Around ten o'clock or a little after I made my way to the pond. There was already a fair amount of people. They were dispersed in little groups walking about the Pond, many of the picnic areas were occupied, and there was a good contingency in the parking area. They add up fast when you start counting heads, I would say a good number more than a hundred. As I made my way down the Pond Trail, I always said "Hello" to the people I would pass, sometimes a brief conversation would follow. One such exchange I learned that the sirens were responding to another homicide within walking distance of the park. "It was a particularly gruesome scene as the victim was decapitated," one elderly gentleman told me. It seemed after talking with more people I was about the only one who didn't know.

Cellphones all around at the ready. I thought of 5G in phrases like "going, going gone!"

I knew they had dropped me as a suspect in the last murder, but I couldn't help but think that they would at least want to talk to me again. The simple life was indeed on a beach in Mexico with Snoop sharing Coronas and talking into shells. After not being able to concentrate on any project I had planned I decided when I saw JJ, I would hit him up for a ride to the police station when we next went to the lab. Maybe I could find something out that would be useful and to let them ask any questions if they had any. All that occupied my simple brain was going to town…hopefully Tuesday morning.

In the woods things were quiet after Sundays rush, a scary quiet save for violent outbursts from disturbed wildlife and the sudden silence after a death screech, or a dark howl. Though the first death was closer to me and I was out of mind at the time this second gruesome murder was establishing a pattern, a new low at which the bar was set. The similarities made it easy to connect the dots and presume these acts were performed by the same individual. With the birds and the fish and all things biologic the staggering numbers of dead permeated the air with ominous odor. Something primal something beyond the stench, an olfactory knowledge that circumvented the cerebral cortex and alerted oneself to a pending doom. Unannounced like a pheromone, demanding immediate action. My cerebral self would rationalize and think and wait.

It got chilly early that evening. I made some tea and got in my bag early. I started making a list of all the things I saw that died. It made you wonder what else had come and gone and of the things you couldn't see like bacteria and fungi. As my list took form, I couldn't help but notice everything was here at the pond, and for the most part was all smaller life forms. I wondered if there was a collapse happening to larger species. I saw some larger birds and some good-sized fish but I had not seen any deer yet. I did count the two people as part of the anomaly but man's inhumanity to man is constant throughout our glimpse into history. The thought then occurred to me that next week after I go to the lab I would go back out to where I entered the woods to the south and go door to door asking farmers if they were losing animals. See if there was an uptick in abnormal behavior.

Staring up at the night sky I extended my middle fingers to SpaceX and the rest of the crusaders and drifted off.

Tuesday rolled around and I went pond side early and waited for JJ. I kept an eye open for species to add to my ominous list. I had found fish and birds, mammals, reptiles and amphibians, I also found grasses, flowering plants, trees and fungi but as my list expanded it was now types of birds, types of fish, species, subspecies and variations. The pending doom hurt my chest, hurt my throat. I could hear JJ's bluegrass music as he rolled in and I was glad I had a prescription for medical banjo. It was administered in the nick of time. I wondered if I was going to surrender to the dread, lay down with the lambs.

JJ was in a great spirit and I needed the positivity and the humor in the trenches.

"How are you?" he asked.

"Good...I think. I've been listing all the dead species I've found and it is getting overwhelming," I told him shouting over the Seldom Scene.

"Details are good but you better back up and look at the whole picture. If you get lost in minutia we might never get to the cause. Stay open minded and have a wide view. If the universe will gift you don't save the birds, save the world."

I appreciated his words and they took me out of the despair and back on the front.

As we got to town, I asked him to take me to the police station first. Officer McCullough was in and I got a few words in.

"Hello! How are you today?"

"Hi, busy," he responded.

"I thought I would check in with you. Anything on those murders?" I asked.

"Funny you ask…I think we found the suspect in the first murder. We should have built a strong enough case by next week to make an arrest. Don't worry, he's not going anywhere he is in the hospital. The second murder no leads as of yet but it definitely wasn't the same guy," he told me and I was glad he shared what he could.

"Have you been noticing all the dead animals and weird occurrences?"

"Yeah, we've been getting a lot of calls. Last week I thought it was just an unusually high number of incidents, but as it increased and continues to rise daily everyone here at the precinct believes we are on the brink of a major reckoning," he answered.

"I've got a couple ideas of my own. I'm no detective but I am going to do what I can," I assured him.

"Good!"

"I am heading over to the lab now…I had some water tested," I said proud of my own efforts.

"Let me know what you find out."

"I will. I'll see you soon."

"Okay you take care now," he said as he was turning around and fetching papers.

I was relieved they caught or at least got a suspect in that first case. It seemed strange that two people were decapitated, but stranger still, two people were cutting people's heads off. JJ was still listening to bluegrass.

"You ever hear Kenny Baker play guitar?" His first question as I got in.

"Oh man, years ago. I haven't even thought about that in years. I've been listening more to Duck Baker on guitar. As far as fiddle players playing guitar love that Mark O'Connor," I said as I was suddenly transfixed, bewitched by the echoes of strings past.

"How did it go in there?" JJ asked.

"Well, they think they found who killed Anthony Petercelli. They haven't made an arrest yet. They also know he couldn't have killed the second victim. He said the phones been busy with people calling about all the weird stuff going on. I got the feeling they know a little more than they are saying," I told him.

"I don't know if that's good or not. Still some murderer on the loose…and the die off is manifesting right before our eyes," he said softly between the banjo and fiddle.

"At least there are a lot more people than just us looking for answers," I reassured him.

"So to the lab?"

"Yeah, we might as well go there first," knowing we had some other stops.

When we got to the lab, it was like another world. Everyone was acting totally normal, it disturbed me. There was no sense of urgency no alarms going off just normal people doing normal jobs. I got to talk to a Steve that was at the counter right inside the door.

He was helpful and seemed to know what was going on in there. I told him who I was and he retrieved my test results. I pulled them out of the envelope and started reading, curious and expecting results. He was very helpful and went through some of the testing that was done. All the samples were in the normal ranges across the board. Pesticides minerals, metals, bacteria on and on zero red flags. I found my little evil sample results and it was the same, no red flags. It was depressing. I thought I failed. I wanted to tell Officer McCullough I had something of importance to share…but I didn't. I still didn't have any answers to the anomalies and now it was going to be harder to find a new approach with my damaged ego.

JJ and I went to a little diner for some breakfast and coffee. It was mid to late morning now so there was plenty of time to shop and get back to my simpler life.

"I just don't understand it, even the water the fish jumped out of was normal, and the spring where the squirrels died, I just don't get it," shaking my head.

"Well we know something is definitely wrong, so let's not focus on ourselves. We can't lose valuable time to failure. Clear your head, sleep on it and see where the stars lead you. There is an answer we just didn't find it yet." Again reassuring and motivating me.

The waitress was too cute and we ordered. She poured us coffee and I smelled it then took a sip. I glanced again at the waitress and asked JJ if I could (God forbid) use his phone.

He had no problem with that. I walked out into the parking lot and called Sarah. "I miss you!" I said as soon as she picked up.

"I miss you too. I have been waiting for you to call or write," she said and it was so good to hear her voice. Memories and emotions flooded in my cerebrum, my heart, my soul.

"So much has been happening. I don't think anyone can live the life more simply. I think I've failed myself but it is not without lessons learned. How are you? How is everyone?"

"I honestly don't know. Things have been getting weird down here. People are going crazy…more than normal, and really crazy. Lots of schizophrenic people committing violent crimes…it's like every day. It seems even the animals are going nuts and I know they're not doing drugs," she said sort of panicking.

"Wow it's the same here. I got arrested for suspicion of murder. They let me go but there were two murders with two victims hacked up…and two different people are suspected of the crimes. I walked by a lake where all the fish jumped out of it in what appears a mass suicide. I've seen birds attacking birds and squirrels kill squirrels. I thought it was just here. Are you seeing more dead trees and shrubs?"

"Maybe a little I haven't been paying to close attention. What do you think is happening?" She asked me nervously.

"I had one idea that something got in the water. I took some samples to a lab and they ran a bunch of tests. The results came back and the water was clean…super clean. I have been trying to figure out where to look next," I told her planting seeds of hope and activism.

"I will keep my eyes open and try to keep notes on what I see. I will ask around and see if we can find a pattern. That may lead us to a cause," she said.

"Good! I am going to have to go…I am on a borrowed phone. I love you, Sarah. I will be in touch soon."

"I love you too. Be safe."

"You too. Love you. Bye."

That was the first I heard her voice since I got here to Massachusetts. I couldn't believe the same crazy problems were happening back home. Being here in a different place it makes it easier to believe strange happenings can occur, but it is hard to picture this same disruption of normal life in my hometown. You do a mental scan of all the houses on the block and try to imagine where the weakness dwells and who will be next to unravel. Perp or victim, perp or victim, who is left to sort it out, who is left to take care of business? With my loved ones at risk I became highly motivated, even more so than I had been. We needed to find answers and fast.

"Thanks!" I said as I handed JJ his phone back.

"No problem, anytime," he said with a mouthful of cream cheese and bagel.

"I think all this crazy shit is happening back home. That's like six hours drive from here. I can't say it's the same but my girlfriend told me there are a lot of more schizophrenic people and a lot more violent crimes being committed. Do you think meth made the fish jump out of the lake or birds attack each other. It would be an easy answer but I don't think so. It must be the same between here and there…that is a lot of real estate, that is a lot of people."

"You should order something," he said waving the waitress back. "Yeah, I'll need it."

"What can I get for you?" she asked.

"Eggs over easy, bacon and a short stack." My go-to diner breakfast.

"Anything else I can get for you? How about some more coffee?" She said with a professional waitress smile and a sparkle in her eye.

"Sure that would be great," I said thinking how much her cheerfulness was welcomed and needed, and how that translates into tip.

After breakfast I went back to find officer McCullough and I did get to tell him that we found nothing in the water that would be of note. I did tell him the samples were extraordinarily pure and we should look into another phenomenon.

Next, we did some shopping, gassed up and were back heading home. JJ was in the zone. We laughed all the way home.

"Hey, you know what a squeegee is?" he asked me.

"Yes. They are for cleaning your windows?" I said not knowing I was being set up.

"It's a short Italian that enforces mob loans?" he said nonchalantly.

"Did you hear about the one-legged European porn star?"

A little surprised I said, "No."

"Lars Hansan Foot and his partner Olga Botvays." I was dying laughing and he continued...

"Speaking of large feet...I've been wearing clown shoes as a penis enlarger...I'm slowly growing into them." And he continued, "Lincoln pulls up in a Volkswagen...and he says...watch me pull a hat out of my Rabbit."

The laughs were just what the doctor ordered. I couldn't believe this serious guy was so funny as he hadn't shown this side before. I tried tossing out a couple of jokes but he knew them all. In the spur of the moment I was drawing complete blanks.

"I got to get right back, my wife's holding down the fort."

We pulled in at the pond and off he drove. There was still a lot of day left and I meandered back to my camp. Having bought extra groceries I didn't stop to collect any plant matter, but I did eye a few specimens that were worth corning back to.

Later as the day wrapped up, I decided it was warm and clear enough to sleep out of my little shelter. And there, even in my few degrees of broken canopy I just had to be reminded of my idiotic quest for a life lived more simply, as a jet flew by, and in the after lull I could see a satellite. As I unfurled my third fingers I thought of my talk with Sarah. I thought how even in a crowded suburb, with all the noise and all the traffic, the family and loved ones were a life more simply lived. With pleasant thoughts of Sarah, I quickly fell off to sleep.

The comfort of my rest ended soon thereafter. As a recurring nightmare gripped me. From my earliest childhood memories, the scarring terror evoked haunts me to this day.

Once again recycled into present consciousness with no loss of acuteness, no use of pastels, or muted horns. The troubling terror was loud and vicious. Never revealing the deep and disturbing secrets this old soul would channel. A part, in the living room of my life, has always been trying to solve the riddle, perhaps a meaningless riddle. Though I was three or four years old when I first had the dream, I can see it as if I saw the movie a thousand times. I ran around hysterically in my sleep, repeating over and over "the ones and the twos married the reds and the blues" and that was wrong, it just could not be! If it was meaningless, it had meaning to me as I spent years thinking about it. At times it consumed me. My life would be pretty meaningless if I let a meaningless dream dictate my rational thought process. The list of representations could fill volumes. One friend once said, "Talk to me in colors, don't talk to me in numbers." But if the ones and the twos married the reds and the blues, one could not separate them. Thoughts of red and blue states, red and blue blood, the entire world of binary existence, from DNA to computer codes. All too deep of thought for a three-year-old's brain, like the clown shoes…I had to grow into it.

Now again the terror had returned. Perhaps it had matured, perhaps I had a new perspective so not to be terrorized by such a simple malfunction of binary overload.

As my window to the ever-expanding universe opened, I could hear calliopes. There was a cacophony, circus music in discord. Notes from the hinter melded with the sounds in one's head. No two notes came from the same proximity. Straining to listen, to keep time tempo, volume or timbre. I tried to hum the melody aloud for reference to keep myself from going mad. But the antagonizing carnival music cut like the edge of the reapers scythe. At times the notes were in my face, loud, other times at the farthest distances from me the sound could be heard. The aggravating concert added to the confusion; the confusion added to the terror.

Enter the harlequin, whose harlequin dreams enticed and beckoned one to the forbidden carnival. As in my youth the simplistic style expressed in an infinite variety would excite to the threshold of seizure. A field of vision maybe four inches square could be cattywampus to fields of vision as large as a galaxy. Flickering between a mile or an acre a foot or a world. A dot would appear on the horizon, in midline, in the anteroposterior of the field and zoom to the closest proximity in the smallest field. Perhaps now it was a red balloon, of no particular size but covering the entire field of vision. Spinning it would move back away from me, and now moving laterally as well. Moving in and out, in and out, larger then smaller. Then up close and small and very distal and enormous.

Shifting positions laterally and superior, inferior, superior, inferior, sinister, dexter. As it moved quickly to the vanishing point two smaller dots appeared dancing in unison with the red "balloon." These too would spin randomly in speed and direction. They appeared to be attached to the red dot but not uniformly as the places of attachment would seem to be different each time, I looked at that particular detail. The spinning and pulsing in and out, up and down, back and forth increased my heart rate and troubled my eyes. In my mind they connected and formed an entire field of vision, then back towards a vanishing point a light year away. As they moved back, they appeared as a triangle, and like a circus performer would cartwheel straight at me and again fill my entire field of vision, the blue dots would gain in size and the red would shrink, and looking again the red was dominant. Suddenly another red dot appeared in the distal periphery and then a blue dot…two, then another red dot and another, pulsing, spinning, cartwheeling. With my eyes closed the carnival would manifest in my psyche. The calliopes recited the clown dirge within the cotton candy of my sanity.

Soon the red balloons started having faces. At first simple, but soon after details, life like faces of that I was familiar with, maybe not all people I knew, but familiar faces from the media, art, television, books, sports. Morphing from one character to another. As I reached to relate, they became people I knew, mother, grandmother, sisters, brothers, father, and friends, girlfriends, cousins, almost everyone I had ever met, returning to that common thread. The blue balloons now attached by long arms were like hands without fingers. Some seemed like long legs and feet with no toes. The limbs would elongate or contract to almost nothing and would vary from each other almost exclusively. There wasn't a position on the head balloon where the limbs could not be attached and so the carnival had seeming infinite freaks on display. Hands and feet, arms and legs, top or bottom, both on right or on left, every face, every red balloon had some freakish quality, within those standards of norms I was the only freak. The terror prevailed.

When I awoke, I felt like I hadn't slept. I felt not only unrested but disturbed.

Something deeply troubling gnawed at me. The ones and the twos, I'd say to myself like a veteran who was accustomed to trivializing the trauma. Right away I made some strong coffee. Starring at my face in the reflection in the coffee in the cup, watching the ripples from my heartbeat and trying, but unable to shut them down. I sat there waiting and thinking for several hours. My conclusion was dreams are bizarre and that was a bizarre dream. And so I struggled with the putting pieces of the dream back together that may give insight or meaning to the carnival of terror.

In the afternoon I collected plant materials for pressing, noticing an unusual amount of dead and dying insects I took some notes and found a few small containers which I easily filled. Of note I saw an ant nest with no survivors, thousands of worms motionless near the edge of the pond, perhaps a dozen larger birds floating dead on the pond…too far out to positively identify. Also of note was a band of trees that appeared dying, pines with dried and brittle needles or no needles at all. The remainder of the day was uneventful.

The relative quiet was appreciated but I kept scratching the itch of that dream.

I was a little reluctant to go to bed that night and sat under the stars with no two congruent thoughts for hours. The dying woods seemed to be gasping for life and its struggles could be heard into the early hours. I cocooned into my bag and prayed for safety and clarity through the night.

The next morning the energy levels were high. Again starting my morning meditations with some strong coffee. I revisited the lab reports and studied them anew. One thing I observed was the stream and pond samples were cleaner than the ground water from the well or one of the springs. One of the springs tested as clean as the pond. I was going to have to take more samples in to the lab. The pond water was noticeably lower in minerals and organic contaminates. How was it possible that the exposed waters were virtually free of the particles that their sources had tested positive for. Where did those contaminants go? By what means were they removed? There wasn't just a mineral testing lower these lower levels were across the board. I was perplexed. Did clean water lead to bad behavior?

To get a fresh perspective I walked/jogged for a good part of the afternoon. I had covered some good distance and a high level of endorphins were released. The vigorous walk back to camp was a great time to slow my thoughts and form more purposeful and direct plans of action. This brain was actively sabotaging my simple. I knew a guy that had a doctorate in spirituality and I could not help but think how that's an oxymoron. That guy was on to something because as soon as he graduated, he went to Nepal. I wondered if his big brain brought him to a place, in a life, more simply lived. We're all traveling in the same direction.

To get back to the lab was top of my list. Making a list of the waters I wanted to check or recheck and then trying to just test a few that I felt would give me the best information for my buck. Two of the previous samples would be tested again. Then I would test a pond further up the road. I was also going to test two samples from town…one of them being tap water…just to see. I was already spending money that I didn't have for this, but it was too important not to.

I wanted to call Sarah again, there was a concern for her and for everybody back home that I didn't feel till we spoke last. Now I wanted to know if things were continuing to unravel, and how many of my family and friends were in trouble.

That night again I had disturbing dreams. In a house where I lived when I was younger some kind of electrical field came in under the roof and raised it for just a moment but you could see the bright flash lingering and traveling back and forth. The wood stove suddenly was lit with a raging fire breathing and chugging like a locomotor. The flu caught fire and in the dream the house burnt to the ground. Unknown people came to help but there was nothing to be done.

When I awoke, though, at first a little disturbed I realized the dream was preparing me-for sudden devastating loss at which one has no control or any warning whatsoever. I was pondering how many attacks we are under at any given time. How few people hold society together. What kind of society would we have if there were no rules or people caring. Somebody would still be alive, but what would they be thinking, what would they be doing? We now are on the brink of war, just had years of an epidemic, the food won't give, the water is poison, and the people are growing violent and unpredictable. Yet if a vestige of sanity remains there is an urgency to help and to fix what is broken. Peace is a dance for only one dancer. Together may we all dance alone.

My simple life again abandoned as I made my way to the highway. There seemed to be an unusual amount of roadkill as I walked east. The cooler temperatures probably led to a slower reaction time. It was only about fifteen minutes before I got a ride. He took me as far as the tum off for Medford. The next ride brought me right into town. The trip to the lab was quick and in minutes I had my sample bottles and was back on the road. Going back to see Officer McCullough I found the station busier than ever. The phones were ringing off the hooks and it was buzzing like a late spring beehive. All sorts of other people were there, filing complaints or suspects or recently arrested. In the madness I was lucky to get a minute with Officer McCullough.

"Looks like you're busy."

"Yes, very. What can I do for you?"

"Any word on Mr. Peterelli?"

"We have someone who has been charged in his murder. Seems like an isolated case. But these isolated cases are becoming more frequent and still may have a common denominator. Looks like a really toxic batch of meth. This guy is totally psychotic and doesn't seem to be coming back around. We're finding this crap all over town, in the bars, in the schools, it's all over…and people aren't just doing it and they're okay the next day…this is the permatweak."

"How did you find the guy?"

"It was Dr. Armich that led us to him. When he did the autopsy, he recognized a particular smell. He thought the victim had the smell of necrotizing fasciitis, a type of flesh-eating bacteria that he had some knowledge of. I don't know how he could distinguish between two different death smells…but he is good. We checked in the area hospitals and found one patient wasting away and near death. Apparently, he was infected when he killed Mr. Peterelli. He had a lot of open sores from his meth habit and was always picking and scratching so it was easy for him to spread it throughout himself. I am sure he didn't have much of an immune response at this time either. He admitted to being very high and not knowing what he was doing, but later realized he horrifically had murdered Anthony Petercelli. It was totally random too, no prior knowledge of him. I am glad that near death he could have enough clarity to confess and conscience to ask forgiveness. That will be up to the Lord."

"Will he have a trial?"

"We don't think he will have that much time. If he pulls through, he will. The District Attorney will have the case open over there until we know."

"So what about the other one?"

"Nothing on that yet."

"I was hoping the water would have showed something…all we got was clean water. I am going to test some more samples, sure has been a lot of weird stuff going on."

"I better get back to it, Thanks for stopping by."

"Thank you for your time."

Before I headed back the usual grocery stop. After asking around I found a relic of an old pay phone in an old drug store. The place was like an old movie and had a counter where they served coffee and old school sodas. I ordered a coffee and called Sarah from the phone at the back of the place.

"Hello Sarah. Are you busy?"

"Hello! No I'm not too busy. How are you?"

"I sure am missing you. They found the guy who did that first killing. He appears to have had a drug induced psychosis. He is now in the hospital near death from a flesh-eating bacteria. They don't expect him to make it."

"Oh my God that is horrible. I am not surprised though. I don't know if it is drugs but people are going mad here. In old town half the stores had their windows broken out, and almost nothing was looted. Over by the highway people were parking their cars right in the road and walking away. Traffic was backed up all the way to the parkway. Some of the people were like zombies grunting and making howling noises, thrashing and gnashing their teeth."

"Has there been a lot more drug busts?"

"Not that I have heard of…seems like something else altogether."

"I am taking more samples to the lab. I just needed to talk to you while I was in town."

"I love you."

"I love you too. Be safe."

"I will. You be safe too. Try to take some notes on what is happening, maybe it will lead us to a cause."

"Okay I will. Anything I should pay attention to?"

"Just be alert and observant. I don't want to cloud a fresh perspective."

"I'll do some investigating, see what the talk is here. Somebody has to have some ideas."

"Good. I love you. I will call you when I get these new samples."

"Peace and love."

I went back to my seat at the counter and sipped my coffee, thinking how, in such a short time since I had left, could the peaceful place I knew from childhood be rolling off the tracks.

The sense of pending doom was real and was affecting me like some…flesh eating bacteria.

The man behind the counter was probably about forty years old. He served me a refill, I thought to myself how it looks like he hasn't been outside in decades. He was pleasant enough, but whenever I see a guy like that its always Norman Bates. I paid my bill and headed home.

It took a little longer than usual to get a ride but the wait was worth it. Funny how things can change in an instant and this was a just such a time. She was one of those girls that could make you stupid in a look. Trying to stay in character was a chore…oh, yeah, I am a hitchhiker. She was dirty blonde, bright blue eyes, full lips and yet not overly made up. To guess, she was probably twenty-two or twenty-three and all woman. Confident and independent, the most dangerous kind of free spirit. As I floundered for words, she had a way that put me to ease, and we talked the whole way back. She told me her name was Rose and that she was finishing up her school. She still lived with her family (Mom, Dad, two brothers, one sister and a cat named Whiskers). Her place was just a few miles past where I was going and she said she liked giving people rides. Inuendo or not I felt as Jimmy Carter once said, "I looked on a lot of women with lust and committed adultery in my heart." She could reel me in without even setting the hook. Right now I wanted to be closer to her and even as the opportunity presented, I managed somehow to think of Sarah. She gave me her phone number and with dreamy eyes and pouty lips said, "It is really nice to meet you, I hope I see you again." I let her know she was the prettiest flower I've seen all spring and I'd like to see her again too.

Everything that was so important that morning seemed to have evaporated as images and sounds of Rose hacked into my apps. My mind played The Wise Maid and Kid on The Mountain and flashed me images of her eyes and lips. Fortune be blessings. As I got back to routine I simmered down and the stimulation made the evening more focused and productive. Plans were laid out to gather the samples and get back to town.

My thoughts bounced from Rose to Sarah and back again and I cursed myself along with the satellites in my life more simply lived. By the time morning came thoughts had returned to things Sarah had said. Maybe they took a day to process, maybe the images were still loading, but the morning brought some clarity to the urgency of her situation. The situation here was the same, only a day away. There must have been people who had seen these events on the news, why wasn't there a mass panic in progress? Were the powers that be aware, did they know what was happening…was it part of some plan?

Imagine Paul Revere riding through the streets yelling "something's happening," not sure of what it was that was going on. That is exactly how I felt.

Being anxious to get back to town I skipped the coffee and gathered the samples. The rides got me there quickly but I wasn't as lucky as yesterday. The last sample I bottled came from the lab itself. The idea of testing the testers appealed to me and I thought it was a reputable place to use as a baseline reference. The lab told me they would do their best to rush these new samples but still it would be several days. I told them I would be back early next week. I asked if they had any unusual results and all they would say was it was unusual for so many samplings coming out so clean. They didn't seem to have a clue or were even overly concerned about the matter. I thought about yelling 'something's happening' but I didn't, and so business continued as it does.

The week passed slowly, anxious for new information, new stimulus, I found myself being extra vigilant, super cognizant, busy to ward off peripheral depression. I couldn't tell if I was in the woods too long or not long enough. Me, my best friend having depression anxiety, nah, he wouldn't do that. I'd better get him back on task. I/We were soon back in sync and back on collecting plant samples. More of the woods seemed sick or dying than my last hike. Browning and withering, even flowers in mid-bloom ceased to thrive. Mosses and lichen too were disappearing and the green carpet by one open spring was all but gone. This had me collecting other than the dead animals and plant samples a new category of premature plant necrosis.

The remainder of the week went by without too much to report. On Sunday a woman was found over by the pond naked, walking and running and babbling incoherently before she waded into the freezing pond. Some good Samaritans came to her rescue. I heard that from the parks guy Daniel. "We get all sorts," he said nervously chuckling.

On Tuesday I went back to get the results from the water samples I brought in the week before. There were more dead or abandoned cars along the road than I had ever seen. Broken fences, cars on lawns, a couple crashed into houses, I guess I saw fifteen by the time I got into town. A couple places along the way I could hear screams, nothing coherent just loud screams.

At the lab Steve was busy as could be. It seems a few other folks wanted water tests done. Everyone was in a sort of panic. Steve said that there were more than twenty suicides over the weekend. People were on edge. Most of the people that took their lives were upright, no history of depression or mental health issues and that was what was most disturbing. People were starting to wonder how they felt…from moment to moment. Not quite sure they were okay.

Every single person I saw was on the phone. Gaming, buying, trading bitcoins, checking the news, the weather, kids walking to school, waiting for the bus, drivers, joggers, at the coffee shop, at the lab, each star burned out and grew insignificant in its own private universe. The apps and the artificial intelligence were stepping into important roles keeping the human species alive and functioning.

Once again Steve told me there was nothing unusual in the samples…other than they were clean, really clean like the last samples. We discussed what other tests they could do there, but he wasn't very encouraging. Finally he mentioned we could look at some samples under an electron microscope at Boston College. This was the first time he hinted at a possibility something could be wrong. Maybe it was just the day after a spike in suicides, maybe something else…but he seemed to encourage me to keep digging, and I felt invigorated once again. I would have to keep my altruism and my ego in check…on a good day I told myself. Steve was great, he knew people there and called and made arrangements for me to meet with one of his professors.

From Walden pond Boston College was only a half hour away. I would need to get samples once again. On my way back I stopped at my favorite little coffee shop and gave JJ a call. I asked if he would be willing to drive me up to Chestnut Hill in Newton. He said he could and we set it up to meet on Thursday. This would give me plenty of time to gather the samples. After ordering a coffee I called Sarah. I let her know how much it bothered me to be calling her after observing all the zombies on their phones earlier in the day. I told her, "At least I was reaching out to something real."

There was panic in her voice. She told me the situation was deteriorating. I hadn't been up on all the news but she said about an hour's drive from her almost every person had jumped out the windows or off the roof of a thirty-six-floor building. I knew where she was talking about, I could picture it…but I could not believe every person jumping to their deaths. She said the random violence and craziness were the new norm, people were afraid to go out, afraid to trust a simple lock on the door. Every one she knew was actively fortifying and isolating. When she said some people, she knew were making Faraday cages it had me connecting the dots. I hadn't thought of the possibilities before because I was so focused on the water. Perhaps this was the epiphany. I asked if she could get out of town, but she didn't want to leave her family. She also didn't think any place was safe, so where could she go? I told her I would be back after this last round of testing. If it did not comfort her, it did provide a wee bit of hope.

On the way back the destruction was even more evident. Wherever your eyes went there was something wrong. Dead animals, dying plants, broken windows, crashed vehicles abandoned vehicles, and people running and screaming. News of the Ukraine, or covid numbers seemed distant and irrelevant. I said a silent prayer. I tried desperately to fill my head with clawhammer banjo music but the situation was more dire.

The samples being secured, JJ showed up seemingly unscathed. We drove laughing and listening to some great old timey music. Singing, "If I lose, let me lose, I don't care how much I lose. I may lose a hundred dollars while I'm trying to win a dime, for my baby she needs money all the time." The whole world needed a laugh even if it was just two guys in a car. Steve had given me good directions and we found the place right away.

The campus seemed quiet for this time of year. Steve's professors name was Doug and it was cool being on a first name basis. Right away I handed over the samples and I don't know how many other things he had going but he said he would take a look at them later in the day. I told him I would come back tomorrow in the late morning. He said that would be good for him. I went back out and told JJ I wanted to get a hotel room for the night as I would meet with Doug tomorrow. He decided to stay in town, as he had some errands to take care of himself. It would also save him having to come back and get me.

Taking full advantage of my room I soaked in the tub till I pruned up. Being so out of touch I turned the news on…it was so depressing…but I couldn't tum the channel, or tum it off. Putin finally got his fifteen seconds of shame. As a human being it is easy to believe the worlds at war, not proud of it though. The sirens could be heard throughout the night. Where was that simple life?

JJ and I checked out and ate breakfast in a nearby place. I really was expecting another disappointment with the samples, but I was still chomping at the bit to hear what Doug had to say. JJ was being funny and I just wasn't having it. I was uncomfortable as rage was creeping in on me. My muscles seemed to be constricting and tense and stronger than usual. I could barely hear what JJ was saying. Water was all I could hear, and I developed an unnatural fear of just a little bit of it. Imagine a lake full of suicidal fish, or cannibal squirrels. I thought of everyone jumping from a high-rise apartment complex, and here I was all of a sudden feeling violent and angry, while trying to practice transcendentalism, each lesson mocking me as I slowly unraveled. Even the simplest life was a burden.

Thoughts of being angry from a toxic liver would make one loud and angry, thoughts of compromised prefrontal from birth defect or trauma leaving me with no way to inhibit my behaviors. I never had these thoughts before except for that one recent night. I told JJ I wasn't feeling well and to keep me in check. He didn't know what I meant but said he would. I hadn't drank in years to speak of and there was no trauma in my life, no known birth defects…I would have known by now if l had. I felt my faculties were diminishing, and I was growing more ignorant as time ticked.

When we got back to the lab, there was buzz. Where it was so quiet yesterday was now full with people. It was like a subway platform at rush hour. The loud and confusing atmosphere was filing through the fetters that contained my rage. "Steady, steady, easy now," I said to myself as I entered his room. Though he was surrounded when I walked in, he noticed and came over to me.

"You are right about that water, something, and I don't know yet what it is…but something is very wrong," he said with an unusual calm in an ocean of dread.

"Do you think the water could be the cause of all the crazy things going on?" I asked.

"We should discuss those incidents to which you are referring. I can see it playing a part, but we don't know how widespread this is or how it will affect other waters," he said.

"What did you see that was wrong?" I asked knowing he was in a hurry to get back to his work.

"It is definitely too early to know anything for certain…but what you left was absolutely insane. I am calling it crazy water for now. There were zero homogenous portions no matter how we sampled it. The molecules were abnormal almost one hundred percent. Basic properties of water were nonexistent, such as the angles the hydrogens are attached to the oxygen, there are some variations but principles do apply, usually they are attached at one hundred- and four-degree angles, we found angles from well below forty degrees clear up to one hundred and eighty degrees. The distance from the oxygen to the hydrogen normally is 95.84 pcm and our findings go from 20 pcm to several hundred, and incredible variations on the same oxygen. This crazy water does not adhere to the basic principles of physics."

"Where do we go from here?" I asked.

"I have only begun and I don't know where we will end up. The deprotonation is frozen up in some of these samples. Almost like it is dead. If a drop is added to some pure water samples slowly, it encases the molecules, alters them and halts the functions. It seems to be driven by a force other than chemically, so we will be looking into magnetic and electric and radioactive cause and effects. I am calling it 'hydrocide' and apoptosis even though it is not biologic I think these terms can be applied to what I am seeing." Doug was being approached by a small crowd and I backed away slowly.

Back in the hall JJ and I were grabbed by a couple of agents. Friendly enough but on a mission.

"In the interest of national security you will have to come with us," the smaller of the two gentlemen said.

After fighting off rage this morning, then hearing about the samples I didn't have much fight left in me. I sort of felt like over-cooked pasta. JJ was still trying to crack jokes… "Did you hear the one about the crazy water," he started. They were not in the mood.

"Where are we going?" I asked.

"You'll know when we get there," the two guys said in unison.

"We appreciate all you have done and we are on your team…but if word gets out and people panic there will be no way to stop the mobs. We just need to buy a little time to look for answers. A lot is at stake, so please bear with us."

JJ and I were both on that page and we didn't need convincing. Let's just hope there were some fast solutions. We were driven in one of those black bullet proof SUVs seems like about two hours to some New England country estate. Old growth hardwoods and rock walls surrounded the place. Down a miles long driveway to an eighteenth-century mansion, stately and modernized for our convenience. Thoughts of I don't want to die here came upon me as I suddenly felt cornered. There was still so many things I wanted to do. We were told we could watch the television but any calls would be fully monitored and zero social media, which was fine by me but I don't think JJ was ready for cold turkey.

JJ and I tried to get comfortable where we were. It would have been great on any other day or any other circumstance, but we still didn't know exactly what was going on. We had everything we needed and some, and though we were willing to do our part we both felt we were being held against our will. We tried to figure out from what Doug had told us…what that really meant. What was going to happen in a day or a week or a year. How did it all get started? How could it be stopped? Was it directly responsible for all the anomalies? If it was going on way down by Sarah, was it going on in China? Sitting, even in some luxury, was driving us mad. It seemed like we should be doing something, anything, but who knew what. Several other people were around the place and none of them knew what was going on. They seemed to take orders and didn't ask questions.

When asked why we were there, they didn't seem to know why. Always pleasant, always "enjoy your stay," "there anything I can get for you?"

Later that evening I asked to make a call and with the protocols being followed I called Sarah. I kept it short and told her I would be helping at the lab for a few days. I said the samples were a little funky so we needed to do more testing and more sampling. In the back of my mind I wanted to yell "RUN!" but I bit my lip and told her, "I love you."

After two days passed JJ and I and two people from the house had the news on. There was no story about the water, at least directly, but along the coast, from Florida to New York more than two million people, maybe much huger numbers, walked into the ocean and drowned. Some went into bays or rivers or lakes and there was no grip on the totals but masses of bodies were floating or washing up on shores. I could smell the death through the television. "Perhaps a simpler life is in our future JJ," I remarked sarcastically. Nobody was laughing.

"We got to go back to the lab," I said to JJ.

"Do you think they will let us?" he replied.

"They have got to, and we better start thinking of getting out of here. Shit's going down," I said.

"Hey, do you think it would be all right if I called the lab?" I asked one of our housemates.

"You know the rules. I think that would be fine," the guard whose name was Mike said.

I didn't know if Doug would be of any help but I asked him and kind of told him we needed to get out of here. I don't know if he felt responsible for us being held or felt he owed me a favor but he said he would see what he could do. The rest of the world had already gone into panic mode and holding us didn't seem to have any point anymore. Sometimes people get locked away and forgot about…! I was glad someone knew we were here from the outside.

In about twenty minutes Mike got a call and was told to drive us back to the lab. He didn't ask questions just followed orders. JJ and I thanked our hosts and loaded up into the SUV. Mike drove and spoke freely on the ride. He said he had been working twelve years for the government and we were just another top-secret story that maybe in his retirement he could write about, and if people didn't believe him, he would send them over to us, lol. He said we were free to go back home and it was a pleasure meeting us both.

He actually thanked us for bringing the samples to be tested.

Back at the lab it looked as if nobody slept since we left. Amazing the stamina and endurance of these highly motivated souls. There was an increase in security on the campus and without our official escort the buildings would have been unapproachable. When I saw Doug, the first words he said were, "It's the posturing dew!" The posturing dew was the new buzz phrase and the entire staff was talking about the crazy waters and the posturing dew.

"What is the posturing dew?" I asked Doug.

"You were here when I first looked at those samples. We saw how abnormal they were, but we didn't really know what that would or could mean in a biologic sense. Since then we have learned so much, but it also gave us an insight into how much we don't know. We have more questions than answers. And with the state of the world we have perhaps very little time to get some of these questions answered. Did you hear the news last night? In what appears as mass suicides, millions of people here on the east coast died. There has been a few people that have survived but their conditions are critical.

"They are mad and hysterical, or froze up with fear or in shock. None of them have been able to speak and no one seems to know how this could have been orchestrated. I am beginning to think the posturing dew has played a leading role in this tragedy."

Doug continued, "The posturing dew is a phrase we came up with here. It refers to all the different forms of individual water molecules. While water molecules are usually dynamic, full of energy and very active, in these samples much of the water is lethargic or even dead. The predominant molecules in these samples seem to be inert. Some of the other molecules seem to be extraordinarily active and seem to have played a role in the hydrocide, the killing of those more passive molecules. Some of these other molecules are hyper, some of them I've labeled manic and their behaviors are bizarre and extreme. Then there is the dark waters, these are the molecules responsible for the hydrocide. They are aggressive and I swear you can feel the evil. Does the micro resemble the macro? Can the crazy make crazy and evil make evil? You are what you eat…or drink."

"That is fascinating. Do you think a person could take on the personality of a dewdrop? How many personality types of water have you encountered at this point? I asked in disbelief."

"Well the molecules are individual, but as types go, I have only witnessed a few different general behaviors. It would take years to go through a few small samples…but think of all the water from oceans to ice formations to rains, if these theories run true there would be about as many as stars in the universe. Imagine the diversity to our species if they could impose their will on us. I took a one cubic centimeter sample of pure water and added just a couple drops of the dark water. Though the water was not alive, I knew I just killed or damned the entire sample. I released the hounds and it was a matter of a couple minutes and the entire sample was influenced by the dark water. It could not protonate or deprotonate, it disassociate and no charge, no pulse. Much of it was like the other samples as far as being inert and frozen in fear. It no longer had any value to the biologic world. And we tested on some cell cultures to look for biologic activity or in this case inactivity and we found cells bloated with water unable to perform the most basic cellular functions. Many cells would continue bringing in water until they exploded. If a person did the same, there would be intracellular water and extracellular water, too much in the blood, hydremia can be fatal, too much elsewhere would lead to the same result. The nonfunctioning of the water leaves the person in a state of hydromania and even though more water would be lethal he still has not met his requirements for living and continues to seek out and consume water. In that condition I would say it would take only about three days to die. I believe now that is why several million people just walked out into the ocean. Thirsty, mad, aggressive, crazy and racing against the clock to find homeostasis."

"Not once in any of their lives was this even an issue and unfortunately no one has an answer. If just a couple drops can kill or paralyze an entire beaker of water and seize the biologic processes of all it comes in contact with, we are in the gravest of situations. Some of the other 'harmless' postures may be well ingrained in our current lives. Without studying these postures we would be wise to find the cause and for humanity as well as the entire biologic world put an end to this dire antagonist."

"Are people tracking and mapping these waters and starting to link these other incidents?" I asked.

"Yes, the entire world is on high alert and the governments are working diligently. From when I first saw the water they were notified and we had people working on it immediately." Doug told me.

"Well, I best leave you to your work. I am not sure what I will do right now but I will be in touch. Stay safe and thank you for all your work," I said.

"Thank you," he said making sure he shook my hand.

JJ and I were apprehensive as we left. We had to have a coffee and a bite to eat. I also had some supplies I would need. Soon we were heading back. It was good to hear some familiar tunes again. We listened to Alex Degrassi and Michael Hedges and then the GD. We were back at the pond before we even discussed the week's events. He said next time we go to town I'm going to pack a bag. I apologized but he wasn't having any of that. "I was with you the whole way," he said.

"Good let's do it again sometime soon," I said jokingly. "I hope everything is cool at home," he said.

"Yeah, I hope so too. Thanks. I will see you soon," I replied, and he was off.

It was early evening when I got back to camp, only to find someone had been there. Stuff was moved around not scattered but rummaged through. I didn't notice anything missing at the time but you can't help feel violated. One has to expect that when there are no locks on the doors…or even doors, and being as stealth as one can be…on public property. Looking around the entire area seemed quiet. The birds were quiet, the animals were absent, I couldn't hear a single car go by. As the night progressed, I made some food and sat up for a few hours after dark. For that time I felt a simpler life. Most of what needed to be shed was caring about all the little things in my life. Maybe it was the dire situation for everyone, but I didn't seem to care about any of my stuff for the moment. I still uncurled my middle fingers when the satellites would go by. Half asleep and caught up in my dreams I thought about Anthony. I thought about coming back to camp bloodied, all the fish jumping out of the lake. When I started thinking about the ones and the twos and the reds and the blues, and then about the crazy water, I thought maybe the dream was a premonition. Maybe it was showing me the state of the waters. My head was so full I didn't know how well I could go back and recover the littlest details, but I rocked back and forth in the dark in deep thought, taking time to ask the universe for direction.

After a while I crawled into my bag and fell off into a deep sleep.

The morning came too soon. There was a dizziness and a residual confusion that persisted through the morning. I ate breakfast and once again headed into town. I needed to see Officer McCullough and let him know what I found out. It was a little nerve wracking not sure who would be feeling how this morning, but I got into town with no problems. I don't know if we were in a bubble, but I didn't see any new wrecks or any people screaming to themselves…and I counted my blessings. There were people out and about but there was a subdued and depressed air on the streets. People walking sluggishly mumbling into their phones, detached and going through the motions.

Officer McCullough was just the opposite. He seemed up for the tasks at hand and I was glad to see he was cognizant and energized. He knew all about the mass suicides and had a few days of 'full moon' activities. I told him about my last few days. "The water was not safe," I said to him. I told him who Doug was and how I met him through Steve. He was calling some of the water hydrocidal and it was wreaking havoc on any samples it came in contact with. I asked him if there were any leads on that other murder. "Nothing," he said.

"Well, if it was just a random act, whoever did it is probably dead already," I told him.

"Doug said exposure to the water would drastically slow biologic functions and people would go crazy needing water that could carry out the essential tasks of life. He said it would take only about three days to die."

"We won't give up on that. Any ideas what is affecting the waters?" he asked.

"Not yet," I said.

"Being so widespread you would think it would be obvious," he said matter of factly.

That is when it hit me. It seemed so obvious and there was no proof. I had been labeled a conspiracy theorist in the past. If ever you point a wagging finger at a corporation or at a given way of life, you are condemned to isolationism and all your paths are uphill. I knew Officer McCullough couldn't provide any proof and it was best to keep it under wraps for now, but once again I believed I was on to something.

"I'll be going now, but I wanted to tell you about the water. Doug thinks that is why all those people committed suicide. I will stop in again. Stay safe!"

"Thanks for coming in. You stay safe too," he said.

I knew there were a lot of conspiracy groups, everyone had an idea of what and who the bad guys were about. Couldn't it just be ignorance, questions that hadn't been asked, realizations that hadn't manifested as of yet. If I were to be productive, I would have to give everyone the benefit of the doubt, and innocent until proven guilty, and then go on to intentions, and motives. All of a sudden, I felt at risk and vulnerable. This widespread will have deep pockets. Swimming against the current is difficult, but swimming against the current and the school is impossible. The only thing worse than David meeting Goliath is David meeting up with a gang of Goliaths. I would need repeating slingshots and divine intervention.

On my way back to the pond I called Sarah again. She told me not far from the house was where the highest number of fatalities happened in the mass suicide. I told her how the infected waters could spread and it was inhibiting basic biologic functions. Then I told her I had some ideas about what may be the cause and I would call her soon when I knew more. I told her I wanted to come home and I wanted to be with her…but I had to at least try to do what I could to help. She knew I was right but it wasn't what she wanted to hear.

"I love you," we said simultaneously.

Next I called JJ and asked if he wanted to go back to Newton. I didn't even ask how things went when he got home or how he was, but he was ready for more adventure. We met early the next morning and made our way back to the lab. I called before we got there so I could get through the security and Doug greeted us and escorted us in.

"What did you find out?" I asked Doug impatiently.

"There is a lot going on here…I can tell you all sorts of things about the water…but not why it's happening."

"Well it seems to be ubiquitous and malignant. To be this widespread it has to be caused by something that is equally as ubiquitous that has to be relatively new to our environment. That narrows the field significantly. To me, and I am no scientist it has to be the relatively recent switch to the five G phone networks. The timing is right and I can't think of any other developments at this large a scope," I said.

"That is an interesting thought. The money is about right too, billions in lobbying, billions in phone sales and tablets, billions in contract for phone service, and billions in new infrastructure." Doug said sounding a bit antiestablishment.

"They'll probably kill you if you try to prove it, and you'll probably die if you don't," I said pretending it was a joke.

"I like the way you think. I don't think I could let the lab in on this. I trust most of my coworkers but this government security is breathing down my neck already. Maybe they know more than they are saying, maybe they are waiting to learn something. They will be watching our every move," he said.

"This is where Steven Seagal starts throwing punches," I joked. "Not yet we haven't said anything," he said.

"So do you think there is something you could look at to give us a hint if we are on the right track? By now someone has had to do some studies on the effects of radio waves and microwaves on water."

"I have read many studies myself and I know there are countless I haven't read. It is very difficult to sort out the information as there are conspiracy folks pumping out misinformation and then the phone and cable companies pumping out misinformation, even the government will sacrifice some of its own for the good of the general public. The truth wouldn't ever get to apply to a single cell or a single lowly water molecule. I do believe there is enough information on the effects to a human cell at this point which would lead us in a direction to look at its impact on one of these lowly water molecules," he said.

"What can I do to help?" I asked.

"Start reading all the studies you can find on the health risks of microwaves and radio waves. See who studied the effects on water. Look at electromagnetic fields and water studies. I remember reading a study on the ionic double layer at the gas bubble/water interface. I seem to recall the water was being affected by the Lorentz force," he told me.

"I know they just figured out why people die at about eighty and it had to do with how many times their DNA was altered. I also heard single and double strand breaks were significantly increased by cell towers. But again I am not a scientist or a conspiracy theorist…why I think I am barely human," he said laughing.

"Let me get back to work. Let me know what you find," he said.

I couldn't help but feel like I just whacked the beehive. JJ and I went to the library and started digging in. In no time we read all the health risks but we don't know who published or funded the studies and what their spin was. When I read changes in neurotransmitters, metabolic changes in calcium ions for instance, that was alarming. I knew a calcium ion is part of the reward system of your brain and a smoker replaces it with a nicotine. The nicotine opens the voltage dependent calcium channels. Could cell phones have the same addictive neurophysiological rat trap? We all know they are addictive but is it more than just gross behaviors?

I felt like my mission was accomplished and Doug would be looking into any possible connections between the five Gs and what was happening down here on earth. JJ and

I headed back where he dropped me off at the pond…back in time(?) to a simpler life. There was nothing that I had been thinking or doing the last, I don't know how long, that Henry David Thoreau would have had any idea. The list was long, horseless carriages, cell phones, radio waves, microwaves, atomic particles, subatomic particles, cell components, indeed we have occupied our time and space and have given great distance to our fundamental biologic roots.

I thought about how my dream could have represented a subatomic particle, and at the same time molecules and I couldn't help but wonder could this fractal have the same dynamics in the excited macrocosm. Could we be just one errant cell going through apoptosis and needing to be shed.

As the night came on the wind picked up. The woods smelled fresh. The wind brought life to the otherwise quiet landscape. There was no simple life, but there were simple moments and here I was, my mind cleared with the winds. More than four hundred thousand cell towers, countless wireless routers, more than two billion subscribers, I looked at myself as the space between the molecules of an emoji. Cascades of ethereal revelations seemed so matter of fact. The fact that memory loss could be traced to cell towers and single and double strand breaks in DNA led me to surmise there was phylogenetic memory loss. Perhaps loss of innate fears, intuition and common sense.

Calcium channels needing to adapt to new postures of calcium ions and searching for homeostasis inside and outside of each cell component are being put to the test. In memory related nerve cells in the ventral tegmental area the dopaminergic neurons record memory of pleasure usually for the advantage of the species. And in my mind, I rattled on about the simplest of life.

"I am not a conspiracy theorist," I said to myself as I climbed into my bag. Like a drowning boy my life presented itself bit by bit. Thoughts went to my family and friends. As I started drifting off, I spied a satellite, and I didn't unfurl my middle fingers and thought of how much I had learned and grown. The sky became silvery bright then I could see flashes and burning objects hurling through the atmosphere. I could feel the earth shake and then shake again. I heard screams and howls then nothing. Entering a tunnel we flocked towards the light.

Epilogue

A thousand years had passed, man was back at meddling with anything he could touch. Each new discovery brought with it a new pathway of fuckery. Once again ignoring common sense and having selective phylogenetic amnesia we were rubbing ourselves raw.

Of note was the discovery of our last demise. With upwards of half a million cell towers and a billion wireless routers the ceaseless and eternal microwaves created a static charge. It was this inordinate static field that attracted the meteors that sealed our fate.

When we prayed to God, our call was dropped.

The Dreamcatchers
of Lago-a-Mar

There was once a great democracy. For a century or two it existed in the ethereal borders where the spiritual and the physical worlds overlapped. Highly functioning intellectuals, under the guidance of a common belief, in unison, brought these self-governing peoples to the apogee of civilization. Throughout the universe, through the ages, these transcendent harmonies nurtured the spirit that tended these thriving cells.

Exclusively, the power of human nature would bring dissonance, and the flatted fifth into the pastoral and utopic harmonies of his own home. As all things shall pass, so this too. Slowly and by attrition had the last nerve been rubbed raw. The democracy had fallen into a state of disrepair and a pernicious autocrat kept his knee on her neck.

Perhaps this would be her last gasp. Blood spilt continually as the revolution and counter-revolution contended for dominance. The just revolution, which championed the archaic democracy, always out-gunned and out-spent by the autocratic powers that be, would cyclically rise to the task and cyclically fall to defeat.

The serpentine network of snakes and rats infested the hallowed halls. Truth became an obstacle to gain, and was shunned. The King of the ophioids arrogantly basked in his corruption. Lusting to print mountains of worthless currency, which leveraged the greedy subservient minions. Power, the excitatory transmitter that rewarded his rancorous soul.

As another revolution was percolating his Lordship would be instigating and provoking. Killings and executions would salt the temperance of the most patient and reserved.

Like a snake shedding skins he would distance himself and deceptively throw blame, often siting contempt for those who had faithfully been so loyal. After a plague of police shootings the masses rioted and sat at the cusp of civil war. Counterrevolutionaries with immunity from prosecution were quick to take arms. Children with assault rifles patrolled streets under the false flag of protection, becoming killers in the unjust counter-revolution. It was in Wisconsin where a couple of protesters were gunned down by an underage teen with illegal weapons. Police did not immediately arrest the active shooter.

Though people died…there were no 'victims'. From the nation's highest office 'thanks and congratulations' were sent out to this fine young man. An invitation was sent so this new recruit could meet and rub elbows with the czar and the animated serpents roosting at his resort. Swelled with honor the youth basked in the golden opportunity.

Driven to be the best patriot possible, he found himself studying history, learning about the demiurge he so blindly worshipped, and deciding on a worthy and appropriate gift to give. Wanting the gift to have deep meaning, not just to the Tsar and his family but to all the kindred loyalists, for many centuries, perhaps until kingdom come. He set about fashioning small willow hoops. For longevity he lacquered them with a fine Shellac of all-natural ingredients. All of his energy, his hopes and prayers went into his work and he wished it would be the best gift anyone ever received. When the lacquer dried and cured, an amber like coating added a nice patina to the willow works. Now he was ready to fashion the rest of the dreamcatchers.

The malleable youth, gift in hand, boarded his flight to Florida. With the glories of knighthood within his grasp, he rehearsed his part over and over again. Say nothing, do nothing, answer only when spoken to, be polite, stand upright, mind your manners, check, check, check. When the plane arrived at the airport, he was immediately met by some of the potentate's men and hurried to the royal helicopter. This was his first taste of the rich and powerful. They flew directly to Lago-A-Mar the domicile/resort oozing with opulence and luxury. To him the king was a larger than life, in fact larger than most lives combined, a sovereign who would throw his weight and not pull back on his punches. He only knew of him what the perceptions were from television, the news and social media. The gilded portrait hung in the halls of his forebrain, humbling and haunting. He repeated to himself, "Inaction, the drill of the divine." Struggling to remember, to practice, to be, breathing deep and full, glimpses of nothing concealed in a jungled landscape of thought, and when all possible dangers had passed, once again 'nothing' would be revealed. The flickering light of Zen, like a store light, obscured comfort, accrued stress, necessitating action.

With several of his men by his side he approached and with all disregard for pomp extended his hand for a handshake and said, "It is really nice to know you."

"It is an honor, sir."

"Don't call me sir," he said friendly like a golfing buddy.

Not being capable of remaining calm and feeling an inch tall, he burst out with 'these are for you,' and handed the gift package over to him.

"We will take a look at that when we get inside," he said.

As they walked across the lawn, he had an arm around the recruits shoulder.

"Glad to have you as part of our team. Please make yourself at home. If you want or need anything, just ask. We treat our special personal guests like royalty," he boasted.

They entered a massive room approximately a hundred and twenty feet by sixty feet with high ceilings. The south wall consisted of polished burl wood at either end for about twenty feet and the rest of the wall was floor to ceiling glass windows, metal frames, of the highest security,with bullet proof, soundproof panes. The coveted views of the primped grounds regally cultivated ego and salted the jealous. Exquisite antiques, museum pieces, throughout the expanse, not overdone but tastefully and functionally set. A magnificent desk centered the north side of the room 'backed by built in bookshelves and cabinets, filled with old volumes and curios.

"This is where I *do* a great deal of my thinking," he said proudly looking over at his desk.

"It is a beautiful desk," he replied without being asked a question. He started to relax and rigidity yielded to a more flexible demeanor.

"Let's take a look at what you have for me," He said.

"Hoping you like them," he responded.

He fumbled with the well wrapped box and inside he found two more, smaller, thinner boxes. As he opened the first the delight lit his eyes and a smile broke out on the usually smile less face.

"These are dreamcatchers that I fashioned from the scalps of those revolutionaries in Wisconsin. The black circle around the circumference signifies they were killed at night. Those dots represent gunshot wounds. Those lines mean they were killed in the streets. Over here is the date," he told him proud as could be.

"You know during the American revolution you would get eight to ten dollars apiece for these. That would be a substantial amount in today's dollars, but the perks these days can be priceless and we found buying loyalty is a one-way dead-end road. But let us keep with tradition and allow me to give you sixteen dollars for the two, as an historic honor from one general to his most decorated liege. I believe ceremony is in order, and not to undervalue your tribute, but to compose in a memorious gesture that bestows honor to your brave and unselfish deed," he said. The sixteen dollars were handed over, adding unfathomable exaggeration to the lengths of the sides of the triangle of God, man and country. At this great length the bonds were weak, and the communication lost, each to themselves.

"I know right where these shall go!" he exclaimed.

Walking over to the windows he said, "I'll put one here," which was about forty feet from the east wall and about eight feet from the floor.

"And the other one right here," which was about forty feet from the west wall and again about eight feet above the floor. His desk was right in the middle of them and directly across the room where he could see them every time, he gazed out the windows.

The dreamcatcher. On the east side had the hair facing into the room, and the other one to the west had the painted side facing in. There they hung; there they were.

That night there was a formal dinner in the dining room, especially for his guest of honor. Many of the loyal cabinet and staff were in attendance, and were there to applaud the immature youth and his reckless valor. Even the most faithful servants did not trust their Lordship and always warily awaited the axe to fall. Too many of their associates and colleagues had been thrown under the bus, missing, disappeared, locked up, or convicted. Not a single one was safe at the Ophiophagus smorgasbord save for the reprieves for the bent or kneeling. The dinner fared well and many connections had been made. He was asked to come again and perhaps he will, after all these now were his people. His fifteen minutes of fame did not have to screech to a halt, thus, cementing his place among the obscure and unknown, rather he intended to milk it as long as it was possible.

Usually the tyrant was amused by politics and polls, loved to play the courts and judges, could not stay away from the spotlights or off the platforms, but today was a day of rare introspection. His mind acute and accelerated, in the void soul a germ of empathy breathed.

From behind his great desk the dreamcatcher to the east beckoned. As he raised his eyes, the scalp captivated and commanded his full attention. Mesmerized and spell bound he sat paralyzed in his throne. He could smell his childhood, hear his mother and slowly streaming all things familiar. The entire time the germ of empathy growing inside. The speed increased and the bits of information extended past his scope and comprehension. As if an autistic God babbled, hyperverbal, and loquacious, the light of truth issued cut upon cut. Without the ability to resist or defend himself the universe continued, every detail, starting with source, trajectory, intensity, duration of each spark of light. Atomic structures and weights, origins of every single atom and molecule. The birth and death of every molecule of water; reincarnations of atom pairings. The specks of dust in all the universes, all dimensions, all realities. The cells functions and activities, every communication between two cells or two cell structures. As the truths flooded in the smallest detail of something personal that directly fed that empathy would be interjected, and again bring his attention to the fore.

His eyes began rapidly blinking as he sank lower in his chair. His hands and face poured sweat and his heart rate continued to climb, but he could not break free, nor would he surrender. If he could intentionally move but one pinky finger or one little toe, he may break free of the paralyzing trance that had imprisoned him.

The hairs on the dreamcatcher stood erect and were oscillating, it slightly whined with a high pitch hum and on occasion crackled like static. The truths received and transmitted by each hair found their focal point across the room exploiting the blitzkrieg, intensifying the onslaught. The scalp with the skull side out was the vortex, the vacuum, which inhaled the essence, and explained the entirety in colors, numbers and purpose. The loudness of war, the quiet of Zen, feelings of plants, every human thought, every emotion, all spoken words, all languages, all unspoken words and gestures, and again he would hear his name. Like the river in Siddhartha the overwhelming cry drowned him, whispering to an om, and sopite slumber. Respite eluded the terminally exhausted. So it continued, every dream ever dreamt, the frenzies of despair in hope, the elusive hope in despair. Each speck of fairy dust on the butterflies wings, where it goes, what it manifests, every grain of pollen, the genetic codes, the life and times of each insect. No rest in his sleep, and then he heard his name again and he jerked his arm and it fell from the desk disturbing his sleep and rescuing him from his trance. Careful not to look back towards the light he swiveled his chair to the left and in a second he was engaged with the dreamcatcher to the west. Spell bound and mesmerized again the scalp commanded the Tzars complete attention. At first, aware and trying to resist, it was just then he felt a strange and eerie presence in the room. From the dreamcatcher to the west, he again heard his name, spoken softly. This time there was a gentleness, a soothing calm, a chilling warmth emanating from his captor. The communications were as slow as spoken word not like the previous overload from the light sabre. He could listen and process all of what was being directed towards him. Though the conversation was one sided it never asked for anything, never demanded any more than his attention. All it had to share was one man's life, one man's experiences, his hopes, his dreams, and as this remnant hung, his nightmares, his fears. Details of his infancy, that the man could not possibly have been cognizant of, but none the less part of his experience, brightly colored and illuminated. Pictures were painted of his family and all the fun times he and his siblings had growing up. All the mischief they would get into. School days and classmates, the details of what any one of them wore on any given day. It was all there and revealed fully and truthfully. And the communications with anyone he had ever spoken to, or anyone that had ever spoken a word to him. The birds, dogs barking, whistles and trains even pins dropping all recorded and playing back. Each step he took, every inch on his skateboards, all the trips in the car, and it poured out, flowing without a valve.

Suddenly, with a loud thud a bird flew into the glass just opposite the desk, breaking the hypnotic trance the king had been under for the last several hours. Free long enough to realize the mounting work he had neglected, evidenced by the clutter on his usually clean and tidy desk. He spun his chair to the north and shook off the repressive mental fetters and slowly stood up. Feeling weak and unsteady he slowly made his way out of the room. In the next room his secretary wondered what he had been doing and reminded him he had an appointment in five minutes. She said she had knocked on the door but he didn't respond and she was about to knock once again. He told her he must have dozed off for a minute and that he had been fighting a headache.

An old friend was his scheduled appointment. He was a known radio celebrity/propaganda minister who had been assigned the gruesome task of distributing opiates. Never short of small talk, never not busting balls said, "The peasants are screaming for more lube, they're fucking dropping like flies."

On a normal day the president would laugh and add to the filthy banter, but on this day, he was more subdued, and though it sounds improbable, his sympathies were with the peasants.

"As I sat in my office, this bird flew right into the window," he said.

Both the propaganda shock jock and even he himself thought that was such an odd thing to say. He had never cared for a pet or even watered a houseplant; empathy was a sign of weakness and that one comment concerned them both. A gentle and subtle shift to the paradigm. The radio host recognized it as an opportunity to ask for favors as the king was at least for the moment visibly soft.

"There are a couple of guys I want you to meet. Maybe put a piece together we can air. One of them is out of Arizona. You'll like him. He always goes the extra mile. He's got a lot of support out there, and they are all for the wall and all. The other guy is out in Texas and you know him, but he could use your help right now. It's a close one there, all that push back. A word or two would go far," he sold him.

"See my people, let them know to schedule me the time with you," he said complacently.

"How did you're meeting with that kid go?"

"I will tell you that's the new look we needed. That is exactly how to make this place great again, a bunch of don't fuck with mes patrolling and mopping up, too young to be accountable, too reckless to be responsible. You can't even draft that shit." He laughed.

The Tsar was not in the least bit amused, but said, "He was a nice young man…I feel sorry for shining the lights on him, I hope it's not too much for him to handle," he said empathetically. Again, leaking traces of compassion, that were visible and staining.

After several many tasks that needed to be dealt with had been taken care of, he had to quench the nagging desire to go back to his office and see if the western dreamcatcher would engage once more.

Entering the room he thought about that misguided bird and glanced over to the window where it struck. The brilliance of the easterly dreamcatcher he was not able to ignore. His initial efforts to disregard failed and he was confined to bondservant for that dangling crown. Back to his desk, at first wide-eyed processing every star in every universe, its origins and duration. The value of anything to anyone at any given time. Where each cent had been spent…any currency, · forever, the browbeating continued. The chemistry of behavior, the behavior of chemistry, each pixel on each screen until it's programmed obsolescence, still slicing and dicing, the unforgiving truth, relentless in the triumphant attack.

Infinite colors, infinite hues, infinite lighting, infinite textures, microscopic fractals imitating the macro, amoeba like paisley swimming and spinning, the strobing effecting seizure, and he clenched and foamed. The cause of every tear, every sexual thought, or act, and again he heard his mother calling out his name, and he saw each bead of sweat. In hysteric convulsion his mind collapsed, the screen went black. The sound of one hand clapping pulsed, spent he fell over his desk, but the light was on…him.

Members of the opposition divided among themselves as to what approach should be taken to salvage the remnant democracy. Some saw civil war as a last hope, though they knew they could not win, they would hope the planted seed would germinate the next time oppression outweighed content. Money could only pacify so many for so long.

Others opted to grin and bear it. Some thought to seek a saboteur to darken the kings dominion, some spewer of sedition to commandeer the air waves and create new realities. As the time passed the oppressed grew more desperate. They were no longer included in their own democracy in which they had been born and raised, built and defended.

It was in Iowa where a scruffy bearded savior appeared miraculously. As the universe was punishing one of its misguided own, it also divinely gifting to one of its own. The universe never lies, but often quotes men, it also never punishes but allows one to suffering accordingly. The hayseed with the overalls was agnostic and apolitical, and as the universe would have it, he was missioned to a small eatery in the periphery of his usual haunts. Sitting at the counter he ordered coffee, oblivious to the fact he was on a mission. Sipping the coffee from his cup he could overhear the men at the table behind him. They were in heated discussion about civil war as opposed to civil disobedience. Ire prodded felonious rage and wrath. He thought if I can hear them so can other people and even if there are the best of intentions, in these days of autocrats and terrorists, you are your own enemy and your own words will convict. If someone picked up a phone, might be the last we hear of them…but you could storm the capitol and, go to your room, no television for a week. He decided he needed to tell them to keep it down and save the threatening language for another time and place, perhaps a little more discreet.

"I would keep it down if I were you. You know they are paying bounties these days," and very quietly he added, "I know a way to get rid of that whole damn batch of them, of them no good bloodsuckers."

They all leaned in to hear more. "Yeah, go on," one said.

"No, no, I'll meet a couple of you out in the corn, right at sundown," he said.

"Don't be wasting our time," one of the men said with disdain.

"Where the Fifteen meets the Three, on the northeast, I'll be there. Safe and discreet," he said.

The next evening as the sun was setting a couple of the men pursued the lead, they pulled over on the Hiawatha Pioneer Trail, where the two state roads meet. There was no one around they scanned up and down both of the roads. Whenever a vehicle came barreling down, they would both get anxious and get lumps in their throats. They hadn't done anything…well maybe they were conspiring…they didn't even know for sure, but none the less they were guilty of intention. God knows what this old farmer had to say?

As the light was fading fast a voice spoke up from the corn. "Here, here," it said with a mellowed gravelly voice.

They drove around the corner, pulled over and exited the truck they were driving. Entering the cornfield the old hayseed quietly and reservedly said, "Good evening. I *am* glad you came. I was not sure if you would."

"We have to give any hope at all a chance," one said.

"You're not cops, or loyalists?" the old man asked.

"You'd be surprised how many reversible jackets I've run into in my time," he cautiously added.

"You would be doing a great service for the people, a great service for the planet. As true defenders of democracy we represent The Peoples Guard. We will keep your identity secret, and the information will be directed in a strict 'need to know' protocol," he was told.

"Now I don't give two shits about politics," he started, "but I do give two shits about this planet. I remember when all this farmland was worked by the people who had a stake in it. They broke their backs for their families, the communities, the country. Hard work didn't scare them. Now as far as you can see corporate farms, and struggling peoples. Yeah, some people still own, I can show you a thousand Titanic's, sinking, mortgages and loans on everything they own, and if ever success, taxed into submission. The banks, insurance companies, all part of the conglomerates and lobbyists and lawyers do all their preaching. They tell you what seed to grow what fertilizers to use. A good farmer was a wizard. He knew things, knew the land, knew the telltale signs of weather and plagues, and had practice methods of solving his unique problems. Now they are downloading digital instructions from their air-conditioned tractor to plant round-up ready seed, so they can poison the rest of your whole state. Lobby me that!" getting more animated as his rant went on.

"Money, does it every time. It can't save anything, can't even save itself," one of the men said.

"It saved some whales once…! I met a rich one that overdosed on plastic," the other joked.

"So you want to get rid of some rats, do you? There is a way and it has worked for a thousand years. You might have to get your hands a little dirty but guaranteed result," the old timer said softly with a gleam in his eye.

They listened attentively to all the details, even taking some notes so they would remember the slightest nuances. As the lights and roar of a truck approached the old farmer disappeared into the dark cornfield. They couldn't believe he was just gone and one called out, but there was only silence and a rustling of corn in the slight breeze. Back in town the rest of the crew wanted to know how it went and if there was anything to the story that the old hayseed had told. "Possibly, we'll have to let you know next week," keeping with the need-to-know policy.

When his lordship awoke, he tried averting his eyes from the beaming truth. Though he could not hear the autistic Gods stream of consciousness, he fought to break the spell, fought to be saved by the human comforts the western dreamcatcher could offer. A ringing phone, a knock on the door, it wouldn't take much. He weakened in the beaming truth. All but beaten down the secretary knocked and gave him the slight advantage. She barely popped her head in the room telling him he should take this call. After several wasted and confusing minutes he was able to once again lock in with the hanging remnants of the man from

Wisconsin. It was as if he reunited with an old friend, and he realized he was more familiar with him than anyone whom he had ever known, his complete life had been revealed, unedited, every detail. The king had always been narcissistic and a greedy liar, and assumed the whole world shared the same selfish ambitions. As the little germ of empathy grew, so did his appreciation for truth. He started to feel and believe there were compassionate people that were capable of seeing beyond themselves, and would give their lives for a better world, for a better model of the human species. From that seed of empathy a sprig of altruism rooted in that enlivened medium.

The dreamcatcher went on downloading the story of a typical American teenager. He could express his beliefs, they were a part of who he came to be, the product of his unique environment. He had come to believe abandonment was a normal part of maturing. He had been left alone to fight the plethora of demons the adults had unleashed. Alone, he found every door he knocked upon seeking compassion, seeking help, had some wage whore fronting a program. Councilors, teachers, doctors, psychiatrists, priests, everyone was paid to care, paid to listen. Friends and family pushed to their own limits had very little time to listen, or spend caring for someone they thought should just "get it together."

The king had made a small fortune selling 'fuck your feelings' shirts and that rhetoric bronzed the autocrats utopian vision. Ubiquitous drugs the 'mine field of the millennials' became the currency of the disenfranchised. Those you would trust most were the ones who sold you out. The world of drugs was so much more than a battlefield, it was the streets, the schools, the mountains and the rivers, it was the world. Even sobriety was merely a measure of use. The culture thrived in court, jail, rehab, doctors' offices. The stench permeated the schools, the churches, the government. The dreamcatcher through his very own existence pled his case, without a spoken word.

The sovereign paid extra close attention to the words and acts he was responsible for in this man's short life. One thought he had transmitted struck a particular nerve in the king, and that was how it is genotypical for a serpent to have a split tongue, and that is exactly how the young man saw the king. Rocketing cartels one minute and hanging the medal of freedom on a known drug kingpin the next. He learned what being a role model was all about and how things he paid no mind whatsoever to influenced and had major impacts on the eager youth. He was ashamed of himself, his lying, his bullying, how dark his everyday had become. The time he had spent beneath the crowns had now become an integral part of his life experience. Whether a blessing or a curse he was gifted an unparalleled acuteness, and access to the universal libraries. He would have to heal, heal from his own shortcomings, and spend the rest of his time and wealth on giving.

In the north trouble was starting. There was concern in Washington that one of his beloved 'rats' was missing. Following the old farmers words, the two men had taken action. They didn't want to implicate or risk another or compromise the mission, it remained secret and was carried out by the two. In war, in just war all is fair, and other lies you've been told. The fate of the 'rat' be it bragging or confessing came to light. The hayseed shared with the men the biodynamic method of the ridding of rodentia, and making sure they do not return.

The men from the cornfield traveled to Washington and stalked and kidnapped the wicked servant of the king. Following the old timers instructions, they were tasked with the skinning of the rat. As cruel and gruesome as the job was, it was done with purpose and conviction. It also minimized the casualties in the just war. So as not to inflict torture and suffering it was done quickly when he was preoccupied and unaware. They shared a sense of duty, and were proud of the fact they didn't bring anyone else into the cold realities of war, or into the heated realm of the criminal. All this, and they still didn't know if it would work. Some research had been done on Steiner and his lectures after the hayseed passed along that information. Driven by the hope of apprehending and corralling the elusive democracy, the work continued. The skin had to be burnt, and specifically when Venus was in Scorpio, this would disrupt the reproduction cycles.

Directing those cosmic forces to manifest their abilities the ashes from the fire, the ashes from the skin were peppered around the capitol. The favorableness diminished and so did the rats ability to survive in that base and fickle environ. Groping women and stealing money lost public appeal. The autocrats' legions faded from the polls. The little people regained their voice. Song once again filled the air. The democracy swaddled every last one, lifting the spirits of the alienated and disenfranchised. Archaic words such as freedom and liberty wielded even more strength as they were resurrected from an almost certain doom. Complacency pricked into vigilance. The weary and the wary kept watchful eyes, prudent to dismiss premature celebration.

Stone soup simmered and they had managed enough for everybody. The capitol was burnt before the primaries. In deciding a new location, the returning of the rats had not been considered. Though the rats were driven out the pipers still piped. Like a virus without a host, the money was itching to infect, and was threatened in its latent dormancy. It was no surprise that the bar would be raised to the bottom line, after all it is the nature of the beast. There was very little time before the effects were obvious. Money spent itself broadcasting, drumming, screaming for the sovereign to lead. With his 'fuck your feelings' attitude Lady Liberty was against the ropes.

Down at Lago-A-Mar there had been some remodeling and redecorating that was done. The office of the king had been deep cleaned and all of its contents had been disinfected and put back in place, with one exception. The scalp to the east now had the hair side facing out of the room. The dreamcatcher to the to the west now had the hair facing into the room. It was not a detail that seemed important to anyone. For months now the king found solace in his silenced friend. It had become routine to enter the office and immediately engage with the man to the west. This day as he entered the office and gazed to the west, he found himself out of his comfort zone. Had his friend betrayed him? Instantly he was bombarded with the ruthless laser truths. The light was exactly the same with which the other dreamcatcher had repeatedly assaulted him. Truths he had come to know, had come to terms with, repeated themselves with the same intensity and brilliance, illuminating unapologetically. The paralyzing hypnotic spell, bound and tormented the one man who was beyond reach. A man did not exist that could be more tortured by truth, more shamed, or humbled. The relentless light beamed. He passed out after a series of seizures; the autistic God continued his hyperverbal ramblings. New ground was covered as he slept. Revelations, crystal clear visions of the future burnt their impressions on his feeble mind. He saw himself as a simple, honest man. A man nobody had a use for, a leader divorced from his dominion, seeking to rectify his lifelong egregious and egocentric behavior.

The next day again he sat as he had for months, at his desk, and risked engaging with the dreamcatcher he had made habit of avoiding, the one to the east. Here he found another man, another life, complete, unedited, articulating every detail, as his friend from Wisconsin had.

Many events in their lives were similar. Family, friends, school, work, drugs, mental health issues…another typical American life. The king listened, he cared, his empathy had grown and matured. To make a country great the least and most insignificant of its citizens had to be great. One man's problems belonged to the society, and each kind word encouraged the faith and love that is the currency of civilization. Yesterday, in his visions of the future he saw himself there, listening, reaching out to the desperate, no longer a leader, no longer perched upon a throne.

He also saw himself after his death, in the hearts and minds of the people he grew immortal, in his death he was larger than life, known and loved by the masses of a great civilization.

The cog of government temporarily set up shop in Virginia. No sooner than having set up shop the rats returned and reinfested the hallowed halls. Businessmen, oligarchs, lobbyists branded their mark on every last particle, and the filthy money infected every living cell. Dualities, right, wrong, left, right, haves and have nots created battlefields, while the money dictated policy and declared the war. Here were the intellectuals, here were the free, here were those who could not sacrifice nor compromise, the infected minions whose programmed behaviors were the capital gains of some corporation.

The sovereign learned the hard way. Now he was vigilant and distanced from the polls and the politics. He was vigilant about avoiding social media and the news. Staying strong enough to resist the bleeding hearts and the saber rattlers. He found a peace that continued cultivating a calm, allowed thoughts to process, plans to be envisioned and executed. While he maintained his office change would only come to him. The world kept spinning; the players played. The last of his legacies in office was the one dearest to him, that brought the real change to him. He started the Dreamcatcher Program. In all the town squares throughout the nation the dreamcatchers of all the people who died from opiates were hung around the perimeters. One hair facing in towards the center, followed by one the hair facing out. People would hear for themselves the truths, in their entirety, and they too would hear the suffering anguish of the human condition.

Other Gods

Bless us, oh Lord, for these thy gifts which we are about to receive from thy bounty through Christ our Lord. Amen. We pray for Richard to make progress in his therapies. We ask for the strength to endure with compassion and civility. We remain vigilant in our eternal quest through Christ our Lord amen.

Meals always began with a prayer. Then a sort of silence would come over the room, which was a modest room, cluttered, and packed with the six of us. It was up to Dad to give the nod and let festivities begin. A rush of clinking and clanging of silver and bowls, plates and cups. The hive buzzed until each had his share of the bounty before him. Mom and Dad would converse about the day's events eating as if it were an end not a mean. Satisfied to savor each and every morsel. Us kids had to be reminded to chew each bite thoroughly. After a few minutes of refueling the horseplay would begin.

The noise and activity would escalate. Kicking under the table, poking, making animal sounds, bzzzzz pinch a bee got you all added to the dynamics of our loving family. When there is an autistic child, the boundary lines of discipline and obedience broaden. Behaviors once forbidden are now endearing.

"How did your appointment with Dr. Schneff go today?" I asked Sarah.

"They suggested meds again, of course I told him that was not an option. Then he suggested "I" take something to help me sleep better and for my "nerves." I wish he would just stop for a minute with the push. I know he means well but he just doesn't get it. We have to go back next week for another assessment."

"I am sick of hearing about meds. What a total lapse of faith. Did he talk about any new theories on the increased incidents of autism?"

"No, we didn't go there."

Charles had excused himself from the table. He was running back and forth, back and forth in the living room. His hyper behavior was always accompanied with hyper-verbally, though seldom distinguishable words were spoken, usually buzzing, humming and dreadful gasps without a break between them filled the air. When everyone was still preoccupied at the table, Charlie was just being Charlie. It was when one had a minute to themselves Charlies activities weighed heavily and were deeply disturbing and depressing. Sadness, shame and unfounded guilt, would be followed by an altruistic savior mode, then denial, recycling infinitum.

"Corn and soybeans were way up today…so was sugar. If prices continue to move up like they have been, we should take the children to France and England before they are all grown. If we don't take the time and make the effort, we will miss the boat."

"That would be wonderful! I will say my prayers and keep my fingers crossed."

"Did I tell you Michael had a heart attack?"

"No. When?"

"About a week ago, he's home now. Sounds like he will be back to working in a couple weeks."

"They want to monitor him for a while and keep him resting. I don't see him all that much anymore but I thought I had told you."

"Dear Lord! If it is not one thing, it is another. That's close to twenty in the last six weeks. One after another makes it hard to keep the faith. Amazing how they keep these people alive these days. I think it was only three deaths, maybe four…Randy, Bruce, Mark. Oh yes and Kathy died."

"So did Will and Lynn. Jesus getting old isn't for the weak. I always remember the old Bill Cosby."

"I don't think it was a surprise to Michael. He has had diabetes for years and still didn't eat right or stop drinking. Never ever exercised always bragging that is how he kept his wealth on him."

"Well you just never know who is next. It sure doesn't seem like how it used to be when only the sick and old were passing. Young people only passed in accidents and in war. Now it seems young healthy happy people dropping left and right."

"It is all lifestyle. People just don't always make good decisions."

"Too much freedom and too many distractions."

"People in general don't plan anymore, they just react. There is just too much stimulus. Rare to find any quiet or even time spent alone."

"The whole of society has gone crazy!"

"May I be excused?" asked Elizabeth.

"Whose turn is it to wash tonight?" Sarah replied.

"Jimmy, I clear tonight," Elizabeth said.

"Is your father done with his meal?"

"Yes, I am done. I may have some dessert later. And yes, you may be excused."

"As soon as you clear off the table right to your homework," Sarah barked like a sergeant.

"I know. Can I please work on my report first, Mom, it is due tomorrow. I will get them done before bed."

"Yes, you better. Do a good job."

"I will. Thanks, Mom."

As she got up from the table you could hear Charlie picking up speed and getting increasingly louder. He had worn out the honeycomb carpet. He burned more energy than the rest of the household. His buzzing was laced with angst and it was frightening to see him that upset and with that much strength.

"Okay Charlie! Let's settle down and get into your pajamas. And get those teeth brushed," Sarah raised her voice to him.

Through his buzzing he managed, "I will, Mom."

When all the kids were in bed and the house had settled down, we could hear Charlie sobbing excessively in his room. Sarah went in to check on him.

"What's wrong baby?" she gently asked.

He was almost hysterical now and couldn't breathe or find his words. His heaving and gasping sank Sarah heart and soul. She couldn't summon the strength for these moments, but carried on knowing collapse was imminent. Now the ghost of dreams guarded unanswered prayer. The 'why me' and life is not fair were treated with a sigh of 'oh well' and a call to duty. Tomorrow's sun knows.

For the next few months there seemed to be a strange anomaly at work. Lawsuits, trade wars, shifting consumer habits would on another planet mean disaster, but the money just kept flowing.

Buying and selling futures, subsides and insurance all played a role in thriving and surviving in an artificial economy. Glyphosate alone should have paralyzed the markets but in these fickle times they continued gaining momentum.

It was on Thanksgiving that I really questioned my worth. The table was neatly set and filled with all that was good and the plates were filled with all that was bountiful and good. We prayed and gave thanks. We had donated food (quite a large amount) to the food bank and to our church which was routine, but a black pall lay across the city. There was no joy, no joy in giving.

After our wonderful meal and a moment to digest Sarah and I went down to the free meal to lend a hand. As I entered into the meal kitchen the sunken eyes of the volunteers struck me like a lightning bolt. Every one of the volunteers looked as if they too were starving! Obese people with boney fingers and dark eyes. Most of the workers had sunken eyes and temples, prominent cheek bones.

We drove back to our suburban refuge. Our table was still full and we sat with our bounty in front of us feeling blessed. The kids joined us and we said a prayed that evening and we prayed for the hungry and the homeless and to all those that lost loved ones and homes in the fires. We ate again beyond our comfort, and left the dishes for the morning.

Charlie paced anxiously in the living room. Tonight there was terror in his face. Wide eyed, buzzing and dancing circles back and forth all around. Elizabeth went in to offer comfort. He was panting and drooling and shaking.

"What is the matter, Charlie?" she asked.

This time Charlie had no delay in his speech or thought process and as if he knew what he was saying, said, "The food won't give! The food won't give! The queen said the food won't give!"

"That's okay, Charlie. It will be okay," she consoled.

"No! No it won't!" Charlie said rocking swiftly back and forth.

Elizabeth started singing. Singing always calmed him down and soon he was humming away with his sister, and soon calm enough to get to sleep.

The following Monday the dinner discussion turned to something Sarah had heard that day on a news show she had been watching. The hospitals, not just locally, but in the entire state were beyond capacity. There were thousands and thousands of people wasting away and thousands more suffering heart attacks and strokes. She said researchers were scrambling to find out the cause.

"This is frightening," Sarah said softly not to raise any more concern than there already was. In the next few weeks to come there was no respite. The body count continued to rise. Tens of thousands of people had already died. Researchers realized people were wasting away but they could not find any specific reason. They too were beginning to suffer from exhaustion, perhaps from the long unrewarded hours perhaps from the universal sense of doom and despair. Up every street and alley even, every life had been touched with the cloak of death. There were bodies lying were they fell.

There was not the time to bury them all. Faith diminished with fellowship and fear took over and isolated the people. Families even lived without trust and turned against themselves. The people, charged, repelled from one another and raised as dust in a landslide into the darkened air.

Sarah and I were managing to hold onto faith, on to each other and on to the children. John our oldest was the first of our family to succumb and he who had been strong and healthy was under ninety pounds when he passed. Up the block it was now in every household, and the moans and whispering cries haunted the landscapes. First there was a call to duty, second was a call of surrender. The fight to survive became a plea for mercy and a begging to die. In the streets there was no looting or fighting. The entire human race was in submission.

"The food won't give!" Charlie urgently reminded us. "The food won't give!"

Suddenly this seemed relevant and important. Charlie had never stopped running about and yelling what we thought was the absurd. And now I wanted to know what he knew.

Scraping the last bit of honey from a plastic bear I offered it to Charlie. "Tell me what the queen told you." I coaxed.

He was morbidly petrified, terrorized yet the words poured from his soul, his old soul and the wisdom was from the fringes of the universe and the cradle of life. The depth of the information and the maturity with which it was delivered made me believe I was not talking to Charlie but I listened carefully to every word as if it were the only option that could save mankind.

And Charlie spoke, "The queen said man is not worthy of the gifts of thy bounty. There exists a higher plane. One in which all living things communicate without words or language or cerebral cortex or egos. A consensus concluded man should no longer be gifted food as had happened before in history, such as the bottleneck on the Y chromosome from about twelve thousand years ago. If a species has the capacity to create a God in its own image and then turn its back on their God and on each other, all the supporting life forms become enablers and his own behaviors become patterns of diminishing hope. Though the fruits at first would give of themselves freely there would no longer be any nutritional value in those gifts. The food the animals would eat would continue to weaken and starve them. Disease would set in as it has from the simplest life forms to the top of the food chain.

"Garlic with no sulfides no resveratrol, no proteins in the wheat and corn and rice. For the foods too were living organisms and they too had Gods that they had to answer to, to be righteous, and motivated to be upright and to carry the light of life and harmonize with the universal melody.

For millennium they served mankind first, who had told them he was the image of God and had rightfully been placed at the top of the chain. It was he who manipulated the crops and domesticated the animals and each and every species complacently fell into the trap, a well-oiled machine of greed and ego.

"There with nothing more than a hope of belief they too suffered until images of their own gods were faint and faded. They had stood by and enabled war after war, even the great one. Watched as nuclear bombs erased the human condition and ended brotherhood. Watched the growth of industries that made industries of their toxic waste and embraced cancer as necessity of a thriving economy. The cars, · computers, cell phones, plastics, non-stop burning of fossil fuels, production of cell disturbing radio waves there are millions of reasons…THE FOOD WILL NOT GIVE! They too have their Gods, their laws and their commandments."

"An apple heard the voice of God, and he was told his enemies would be delivered over. Though he was weakened too he believed and was willing to sacrifice knowing too his kingdom was at hand. It was from that first seed that the plants held firm to their convictions and refused to serve up any molecule of nutritional value. It exponentially spread through every species and to every comer of the earth."

My mouth gaped open as I was astonished. Did my littlest child have. Divinity? Another day perhaps I would think he was crazy but millions of people were dying. Now! Right before our faces…

"Did she tell you what we can do about it?" I asked.

"No. There is Nothing we can do. The Food will not give!"

"Thank you, Charlie. Perhaps now we have a point to work from and a direction to go. Let us not give up our hopes and beliefs we too have a kingdom worth sacrificing for. No matter what happens know that I love you."

The end was now in sight. Without nutrition bodies fed off of themselves. Soon the fat in the brain would be reduced and so too man's ability to organize, plan and execute. Language would slowly disappear; whole categories of words would go extinct in just a few weeks. Jargon, technical terms, mechanical terms, cooking lingo, entertainment, lyrics, religion, philosophy, medicine, history, all reduced to a few grunted consonants. Pages of books were eaten along with their leather bindings. None was saved. No glimmer of hope of future.

Cities great and thriving just months ago stank of the rotting corpses not just of man but of his animals too. The cattle, swine, sheep and goats from the rural areas into the suburbs. The pets of cats and dogs and the birds in the cages within the boundaries of the cities of them none remained. And none so ever laid torch to the cities, not even did the waters run. Silence was deaths comrade and the wind did not blow and the sun bore down. The wailing and weeping and gnashing of teeth made no memories. From the lands that sat along the great sea to the west to the lands that sat along the great seas to the east and across the two great seas to the lands beyond they too were silent and dead. There were none to mourn and man's gods looked elsewhere for praise and gratitude. They too were dying…without parade or fanfare.

Though it was probably too late it was time to act. I didn't know my lines. The whole world…stage fright. I called emergency services, police, fire departments, looking for a vein that was still functioning. I called newspapers Television stations, radio stations and this is where I found a faint heartbeat. Of course the world was in dire need for answers and only perhaps I could help identify the problem. There were ears and I delivered to the dwindling multitude. Many man, woman and child passed comforted with the newfound hope. The desperate and bleak message entrenched those soldiers in their faith. None looked for a new faith.

The radio stations phones rang off the hook, as did mine. It was less than twenty-four hours later Washington sent people to retrieve Charlie and myself. The president wanted Charlie close to him…not just for answers but for protection. He couldn't take unnecessary risks with a Messiah(?).

When the secret service knocked, there was a sense of pride and patriotism, humanitarianism rushing through me. I felt important and for a few moments I allowed myself.

Sarah was staying behind with the other children. Elizabeth was suffering and extremely weak. In constant prayer with life on the cusp.

"I love you! We will be back soon," I assured her.

"Please don't be gone long. I don't know what we will do without you," she said squeezing me as if it were the last time.

"Are you ready, Charlie?" I asked.

Looking over I could see Charlie rocking back and forth shaking and crying and between gulps and sobs managed a "NO!"

"Come on Charlie let's get your bags. Everybody needs you. You are a very important person," Sarah convincingly coaxed.

Charlie mumbled, "The food won't give," between gulps and gasps. He grabbed a bag and kissed his mom and headed out the door.

The family waved from the porch as we loaded into a big black sedan and headed off to the airstrip. Charlie was almost getting comfortable with himself in the state of pending doom, the panic from the rest of the world, the hopes and heartbreaks were unbearable.

On the next day it was about ten o'clock am when we met with the president. Though I was still riding high on being important I realized I had nothing to do with any of it. The president was cordial but working way too hard on being Charlie's friend. He had lost a lot of weight from when I had last seen him on the television. He was fragile and frazzled and desperate.

"Did you enjoy flying?" he asked Charlie.

"Yes sir," he politely responded. "Though I would rather be home," he added a moment later.

"Soon enough," he guaranteed.

"Shall we take it out to the garden?" he suggested as he was heading out of the room.

"I will get us some refreshments. How does iced tea sound?"

"Thank you," I stiffly replied.

The president wasted no time getting down to business. He asked Charlie to tell him any of the tiniest details that might have a clue to the answers so desperately needed.

"How did you hear this message? How were you able to talk to a bee? Did the bee tell you where she got her information? Did she tell you what we can do to stop this? When was the first time you spoke to the bees?"

Charlie listened to the president with great respect and answered what he could. At the end of several hours no progress had actually been made. The president heard a very fascinating story that he wasn't sure he believed fully which ended with, "The food won't give!"

The president's demeanor eroded and he had a couple of his men escort us back to our room. "I will see you again in the morning," he ordered.

As we sat in the room, I was feeling like this was all a mistake. Charlie did not want to be here. The rest of the family was needing us. The president was wallowing in his own insecurities and the immediate situation felt volatile. I tried not to let my fears escape and it was easy to distract Charlie by looking at the problems of the whole world. He was a trooper and had resigned himself to the powers that be.

Back at home the middle-class life was unraveling. Elizabeth was fading fast. Sarah was at her wits end. Prayers were thrown into the pond without so much as a ripple. James couldn't take it anymore…first was loud and angry, then resolute with a contingency.

"I am not going to die!" he told his mom.

"I am not just going to wait here and watch everyone die waiting for my turn. I am getting out of here…I am getting out."

Sarah tried to convince him otherwise but he was mad with determination.

"I am sorry, Mom. I want to live!"

She knew at this point she couldn't stop him and really didn't want to. Maybe he had a chance maybe something was driving him intuitively or divinely just maybe there was a hope incubating.

"Where will you go?" she asked.

"I don't know. I think to the mountains away from all the people. Where I can hear God and he will talk direct to me. Away from all the suffering," he said as he packed a backpack with his collection of survival gear.

He went in and said his goodbyes to Elizabeth who encouraged him with sunken eyes and dried lips. "You be safe. Live for all of us. I love you!"

"I love you too! Get well! I will be back!" Seeing her like this was too much after John had passed and he knew how it would progress.

He said goodbye to Mom and for the first time in his life he was lost and alone and he knew it. And James moved on, one foot in front of another. It was too late to live, too early to die. The roads were quiet and still. Cluttered with useless automobiles, abandoned or else a tomb. The putrid smell of hot boxed rotting flesh slow roasting in the California sun. They can't get me he kept saying to himself. I have important things to do.

James crossed the river on the bridge then moved easterly along its bank. Time became unimportant but night overtook him. Darkness was exhaustion's companion. He collapsed in the hollow of a redwood and made a pallet of the needles and duff thereof. Only a few short hours of respite then the haunts and terrors dominated whether he lay awake or fell to dream. It was still dark when he prepared for the day. The few bites he ate left a lump in his throat. He swallowed a spoon or so of dirt and washed it down with some questionable water.

He remembered seeing John as he lay emaciated, dying and yet so full of bright things…ideas, imagination, love and hope, and a belief in eternity. Fear and wickedness nonexistent and James prayed for that wisdom and strength. He whid on along the south bank. There was an ominous peace in the forests and fields and an ominous sense of doom where the people had been. A car, a house, a little village all knotted his stomach and produced great anxiety. As he continued his trek, he preferred to avoid signs of man as best as he could. Though the frequently traveled routes made for better 'time' as if that mattered.

The wrath was friendless and needed no allies. It made no exceptions and no exclusions. God lost face and form, no longer in man's image. But on the tip of his tongue, the faithless and the faithful with curse and prayer cried out to strange Gods as he gave up the ghost.

The hive was a buzz in Washington. Insanity was widespread. Failures to report from the cabinet left the administration hollering at empty halls. No data from the scientific, economic, academic, health or military communities. Skeletal remains of each and every branch of government.

The president was impatient that morning as his grip was failing.

"God damn it! We don't have much time," he said looking straight at me and talking to Charlie. "How do we get a message out to them? There has to be some way to negotiate, some compromise. I will do anything, whatever it takes."

Charlie calmly resigned himself to the facts and said, "The food won't give."

This further enraged the president and day two of our peace talks reached an impasse. The president was flailing his arms. "This is unacceptable. I told you we need answers. God damn nasty people!" We were ushered out and once again held in our room. We heard him cursing and stomping around his office as we exited. I wasn't proud of his parenting skills or his leadership skills under pressure. Looking at my son I was embarrassed for the whole lot of us, ashamed of the whole process.

Sarah called after we were back and let me know how dire Elizabeth's condition was at his point. She could hardly take water. She knew it was now only a matter of hours. She held the phone to her ear and I told her how much I love her. I sang to her as she had to Charlie. I put Charlie on for a minute also and he said, "Don't be sad. I will see you tomorrow."

I told Sarah how our talks were not going like I hoped they would be going and the president was acting like a spoiled kid. There wasn't much we could offer and Charlie just kept saying "the food won't give!" She begged us to come home. I told her, "We would be home soon. I love you! Keep praying!"

Even in Washington the bodies lay where they fell. Rotted flesh around gaping mouths as if they begged for food when darkness came to light. Silence echoed the moans of suffering. Through famine and disease civility vanished. From the great institutions to a simple act of kindness the righteousness of man no longer existed. Countless Gods created and abandoned each wore the face of death. Once again in man's illustrious journey children became prey. Though sickly women bore sickly children there was still a calorie of hope therein and all fair game on the brink.

As night came on it appeared to be night for all of life. The render garments of the reaper had brushed the wisps of breath from us all. I knew when the phone rang one more time that night death had come home and a completely broken Sarah relayed to me the death of our daughter Elizabeth. As the suffering became unbearable something was breaking inside of me. I too just wanted to go. To surrender to whatever it was that would come next. The world didn't seem worth saving and I wallowed tormented in pity surrounded by pitiful people looking for just one eye with a light turned on. My weakened heartbeat still louder than all the voices in the world separated me from the OM. Perhaps this shadow of ego was all one needed.

Early the next morning Charlie and I were collected to meet again with the president. Charlie was in an uncontrollable state. Terror was in his face and on his lips. I assured him things were going to be fine. I let him know we were doing our best to try to save the world.

"No Dad, it's over," he whispered.

I had my arm around his shoulder and whispered back, "Superheroes must keep going."

We entered the Oval Office with our escorts. There were several other people in the room. We were not introduced and the president looked like a mad dog. Pacing back and forth behind the large desk of importance. His jacket was off and tie loosened, sleeves partially rolled up. Curse words were all he could muster when he addressed his thin loyal staff. And I wrapped up with my loss. My son, my daughter and it was driving me to the edge. Perhaps I felt the suffering of the world at large, the suffering of every family, the loss of our way of life, of civility, of compassion, of hope. The president was wrapped up with his loss too, of power and control. He could not snap his fingers or jump up and down like a spoiled child. His cursing and screaming had no reaction, no ears. Not once did he have the air or appearance of a leader. Not once a speck of altruism. Not once any sign the people rose him up to be the supreme voice, the unwavering truth, the brave and fearless beacon. The little man with the giant ego managed to put a fork in the sacred ideals and the moral compass of my entire life. I was tired. I was suffering. I did not want to reduce myself to his level. I did not want to die hating, hating everybody and everything and every minute of my foolish life. I looked at Charlie and I loved him and I knew I loved him and that separated me from all the lost souls in the room. I breathed deep and relaxed remembering my purpose, appreciating myself.

"So what can you tell me?" the president barked. "The food won't give." Charlie said.

"God damn it. I know that. Tell me fucking something we can use. I don't have time for this bullshit!" the salted slug screamed.

"It's too late. The food won't give!" Charlie added as if to comfort him.

"Get them out of here!" he bellowed.

And as two of the president's men approached us aggressively, I turned and looked at them and in the comer of my eye I saw the president run his hand passed his neckline in an off with their heads gesture. I swallowed and felt my heart sink. I put my arm around Charlie's shoulder and we left the room.

Before we got back to the room where we had been staying three men walked down the hall towards us. I was uneasy but still not prepared for the reality of the situation. The two secret service escorts continued down the hall with my son and I was physically assaulted and detained. I had been struck in the head and though I don't think I lost consciousness by the time I got my wits about me Charlie had vanished from my sight. As I struggled, I was taught lessons in pain and submission. My threshold was high so they went the extra mile. I wasn't sure why we had been separated but all my scenarios were ominous. I had to get back to my son. I had to make sure he was safe.

For James another day passed and another victory. Further up the river ever moving upward.

Always aware of the fact he was denying his own death, believing he was defying his own God. On this morning he was the jackal, he was the vulture. His stomach growled and his desperation grew. All he could think about was food. He remembered Thanksgiving dinners, the table filled with food with even more food waiting in the wings. He lusted and salivated. He smelled the turkey and imagined the mashed potatoes with a lake of gravy.

He came to a place far up the river where three creeks converged and gave life to the river. The middle fork was the more substantial so he made his way over to its south bank. It was no more than a mile upstream he found a young mother and her infant who also tried to outpace the inevitable. He could see she was once stunningly beautiful and how death when it came was her salvation. James thought how dignified to surrender with such comfort and to wear that eternal peace on her face. He assumed the infant had died first for then she might wear the mask of terror.

James knew he wasn't going to meet the same fate. Always the opportunist he reached down into the mothers arm and removed the infant. He examined it and smelled it. He sliced it from the backside like a ham. Though there wasn't much meat there was enough. He built a small fire not that he needed a hot meal but to make sure he killed any parasites or pathogens. His mouth continued salivating as he seared the steaks. He never asked forgiveness or said thanks. Grace was not said. This meal had not been blessed. As he took the first bite, he realized he had embraced an evil he had never known. He slowly chewed a couple of times but he knew he couldn't swallow it. He thought I have to sustain myself and chewed again for a second. His empty stomach was coming up and he spit it out without swallowing. The manna that had been gifted had been refused. Perhaps the gift was the knowledge of what he could and could not live with. One bows out when the rules of the game made it so you did not want to play.

He thought of how he read and reread Siddhartha as a boy, a Brahmin, a Samana, a womanizer, a gambler, a ferryman. Perhaps I am just another voice in the river. I can think. I can wait. I can FAST. He breathed like a yogi, full breaths. He stayed focused on breathing full for some time. There were people who had lived entirely on breath and water and that thought came back to him as he meditated on breathing. Breatharians, it sounded bizarre and yet it seemed to be necessity. And if the light and air provided enough prana enough vitality there was a chance something of mankind could be salvaged.

Onward and upward scrambling on the rocky creek bed. The landscape started to level out in a grassy alpine meadow. The view upstream was the most majestic he had ever experienced. The tallest mountains he had ever witnessed gleaming with sunlit fields of snow. To the north and the south giant mountains framed the postcard. A sense of satisfaction filled his soul. There was a sense of "I made it." Even the shallow hollow victory to the narcissist was worthy of celebration. He paused, he breathed.

For a moment he puffed out his chest and became altruistic, humanitarian…for a moment. Realizing how alone he was he continued on.

The room I had been left in was small and dark. The door had been locked. My urgent need to get to Charlie triggered a claustrophobic attack. I fought the panic and tried to control my breathing as the room closed in around me. I can think, I can think, I can think. A meaningless mantra if ones not thinking. I pounded on the door, yelling, not sure that if anyone heard me, they would help. As I lit my lighter, I noticed an electrical outlet and I worked on that one weakness in the defense. Removing the plate and the junction box I started working on the wall in the back and prying away at the wall in front of me. Once the hole was big enough, I could kick out the wall in the next room over. It didn't take long and I was at least out of my cell. Quietly I moved towards the large windows on the other side of the room from the doors. I knew there would be alarms but for some reason I thought it better to move about from the outside. As I stood behind the drapes looking for a latch, I saw Charlie in the courtyard crying, screaming, "Mom, Dad, Mom." The thugs who had taken him were there hitting him telling him to shut the fuck up. One delivered a strong right knocking him down and the other pulled a .38 and execution style shot him in the back of the head. There was nothing that could be done and my hopeless self-basted in my own boiling blood.

My fate would be the same if I didn't get out of here. Making my way back to the door I cracked it and looked down the hall. It was so quiet, so deathly quiet. Without seeing a soul I made my way outside. I wished I'd lit the place up and escaped as if I were in an action movie…but it was deathly quiet and I was doomed to live. Without attracting any attention I went around to the back in the surreal dream state of trauma. The anger could not be contained within me. There was no place for it anywhere, not in this life nor the next. Perhaps the anger was all I was living on at this point. All my fire all my fuel. I thought of Sarah and had to get back to her if it was the last thing I do. I needed her, her warmth, her smile, her gentle voice. Sprinting I made my way across the South Lawn. There was absolutely no resistance in fact there was nobody except for the corpses that lay here and there along my path.

By the time I reached Constitution Avenue, I had slowed down to a panicked jog, due west with Sarah on my mind passed the United States Institute of Peace. Soon the Potomac River was before me. The OM had been silenced by the microcosm of self. Maybe the river was my friend, I believed it was but I did not take the time to make it's acquaintance. Right now it appeared to me as an obstacle and all I wanted to do was to get home. Traveling north along the east side of the river I made it to the Francis Scott Key Memorial Bridge, which I traversed in double time. Continuing on northwest along the west bank I found myself traveling on the Potomac Heritage Trail. Thirty hours must have passed before I collapsed and fell into a deep sleep. There was no way to tell how far I had traveled; I only knew what country lay in front of me.

The sun was beating down on me when I awoke. I regretted the time I spent sleeping and made haste. Again, thoughts of Sarah and Charlie made my heart pound fierce and loud. There was a little boat house up the way and I took the liberty of commandeering a small boat and motor. They were beckoning and seemed to be offering comfort. The few live people I saw were fighting and I hurried by and tried to disappear. I knew I had to eat something. I was losing my abilities to plan and execute.

There must be fish in the river I thought but I let the motor just drone on.

James had been continuing south along the well-developed trails of the Sierras. Dropping in and out of watersheds. His being alone provided a different sort of peace a different sense of strength. He was no longer hungry and felt empowered by his breathing regiment. He felt godlike in his ability to survive. There was no specific destination but he knew he would be away from most of the people in the high mountains. He had been thinking of a trip he once took hiking around Sequoia Park and south down to Mineral King. It made sense to migrate south to warmer climates knowing how thorough the die off has been. By winter he could climb down off of the mountains and at least stay a little warmer.

The alpine lakes were spectacular even in times of distress they had a calming effect. The majestic mountains had the ability to make a life…any life seem so insignificant. So close to heaven one could reach out and touch it. So close not so much physically but spiritually and emotionally. If one were to die, this would be a good place and a good mindset. Eagle Lake was the appropriate name of the spot where he landed this particular evening. As he stared out across the perfectly still and picturesque lake, that reflected every bit of the jagged peaks and talus slopes that surrounded, he saw a small human figure across the lake. Approaching from the rocky gorge the outlet had chiseled over the many millennium. A cascade of thoughts bombarded and he ran through the faces of almost everyone he ever knew. He focused on his mom and dad and his brothers and sister.

Though I was met with some difficulties along the way I had managed to make my way up the Potomac to a place called Falling Waters. My eyes and my mind played tricks on me, from blind to perfect vision in both the micro and the macro. Sarah must still be here. I could feel her. As I lay on the grassy bank something was lifted from me and the urgency of the fight became subdued. Sarah was still front and center in my mind as the candle grew dimmer. All this because of some other Gods. Perhaps I was growing mad but I couldn't help laughing, thinking of Charlie telling the president, "The food won't give…there is nothing we can do…the food won't give." Other Gods indeed. Drifting off realizing I was locked into the binary code of my mundane existence. Even my beliefs were nescient. I longed for enlightenment and embraced darkness. The nearer death the further light. Poisoned with the ignorance of dualities I clung fast to my own essence. Light dark, life death, love hate and as I meditated towards Brahmin, I would find myself asking Jesus for help and guidance. Weak ignorant, childlike I wanted there to be a heaven and hell. I wanted to go to Disneyland in the hereafter, stroll the arboretums of eternity.

Curled up, the little light left in me flickered. I thought of Sarah again with my whole being, praying she would survive. How verily Brahmin this all Is. Once again, I found myself praying to Jesus, for Sarah for Charlie for James. Again I fell in the trap of ignorance and duality. As I contemplated my dilemma a vision of the presidents head taking up three quarters of my visual field came floating at me with the Theme from Jaws aggravating my inner peace. I cursed, cursed at the other Gods, cursed at myself, my ignorance, cursed my last thought and feelings to carry into the unknown hereafter would be that of hate. It was those feelings and thoughts that burned the rest of me and the light went out.

Sarah immediately knew I was gone. This was more than she could bear. All of her children were gone and now her husband. The darkened streets bode a certain death. Hope was futile. Against all her beliefs in an effort to reunite with her loved ones Sarah broke her own sense of morality and consumed a lethal dose of the prescription medicines she had on hand for John and Elizabeth. James felt his mother leaving and somehow knew she was the last of his family. He remained determined and defiant.

James could now see the figure was female. She was thin and unsteady in her gait. James walked over to her and helped her to his spot on the other side of the lake.

"I am James," he said.

She didn't introduce herself but weakly said, "Everyone is dead."

"You haven't seen anybody?" James asked.

"No, not a soul," she replied.

"It sure is wonderful to meet you, I was afraid I would never see another living person."

"I just want to die!" she snarled.

"No, we have great responsibilities, great possibilities. You are the queen of the earth. What is your name, Your Highness?"

This struck a chord with her and it was the first time she can really remember being appreciated. "My name is Evelyn," she quietly answered.

"I will call you Eve if that's okay."

She didn't know why she had started walking. Everything she had known was dead, everybody. As far back as she could remember all she ever wanted to do was die, and yet she was doomed to a long life. Her behaviors accented the abuses she was too young to remember. The betrayals of family, of authorities, whom later she was supposed to trust. Those stained pillars of society that looked the other way when she was defiled and reaching out for help. At a toddler's age, her mother's friends played with her in exchange for drugs. For months at a time she survived on methamphetamine, semen and beer, while her unconcerned strung-out mother entertained in the other room. One after another Mom's friends made their mark on her. After years of violence and abuse, a hero came and rescued her, she was all of eight years old. Emaciated and near death she was hospitalized and after months regained some strength, but never emotionally or mentally. She assumed all this was normal and no one could tell her otherwise. As she grew up, all she wanted to do was die. From sexual damage and from disease she was told she would never have children. It had always been difficult to put cerebral pursuits above biologic necessity, in her cognizant moments it was possible but any weakness at all opened a floodgate of depression and suicide.

She had kept walking, nowhere, but kept walking. Men war, women endure she thought.

Bastards they are all bastards. Again, in her short little life she was saying, "Why can't I die? I just want to fucking die." As she climbed beyond the towns following patches of wildflowers she looked back over the silent expanse. Birds weren't singing, crickets not chirping, no planes in the skies, not a motor purring, only the gulping and gurgling of a small creek and an occasional breeze that would rustle the leaves. For a brave moment she thought maybe I could handle living if all the bastards were gone. But soon fear got to her and her reactionary self-wanted out. Every breath in she whispered "fuck" and every breath out a silent sigh. Through the thick dark forests to the lush alpine meadows she marched, surviving without purpose. A string of six peeks across the pastoral meadows beyond the talus slopes beckoned. And she cursed her way towards them weak and crazy.

Now all of a sudden things were a bit different. It was going to take some time to process and make adjustments. So free of judgment, of rules, free of standards, free of people.

James again called her the "Queen." And she felt a genuine sincerity and for the first time she didn't feel like she had to kill someone or run and hide.

"I should teach you to breathe," he said. "We can get all our prana from light and air. And sustain ourselves until we have more knowledge of our situation."

As they practiced breathing together miracles were happening. And though James had only known his arrogant ways a warmth of empathy awakened him to others perspectives. And for the first time in his entire existence could he view himself as a stranger. Not being mentioned to him, nor did he ever realize it himself, all his life he had been cursed. And not once in her entire life did she realize she had been blessed.

They breathed together and held each other through the night…and she didn't hate…and he could love. In the cold predawn they watched the moon set behind them as they hiked up to the summit of an unknown fourteener. Along the meadows edge Eve spied an apple tree and plucked the forbidden fruit. She polished it as they climbed further and further up towards the top racing the early sun. It was a new day, a new beginning and though it may take many lifetimes to forget the past this day a new love flourished. James facing the east raised his arms to his sides to hold all of the universe he could manage and in doing so his shadow formed a cross on the rocky ground behind him. And Eve seeing this fell to her knees about the cross and honored it with the offering of a rose. From this moment on she was whole again. The fruit of her womb was bountiful. The apple she had held on to she finally took a bite and was satisfied. As some other God had delivered up the enemy and man was no longer at the apex of the food chain. No longer would he be childlike and egocentrical. No longer would the Garden of Eden need conquering.

Of these we do know, perhaps there were others and other Gods.